Avi Gvili is a writer, educator and playwright. His previous books include the popular **Samson Turner & the Legend of Hercul**es as well as the short story collection, **Life & Love & the Like: Stories from the Everyday.** His produced plays include **The Fiendish Fiends, A Key for all Ages, and A Question of Religion.** For over two decades Avi has worked as an English Teacher in NYC schools. He lives in Staten Island, NY with his wife Helena and son Ethan. Visit him at avigvili.com and boulevardbooks.org

The Quest for Olympus

Book II

The Samson Turner Saga

By Avi Gvili

TABLE OF CONTENTS

Chapter 1

The Man in the Hood

I t was in the nighttime that I became afraid of my dreams.

The man — if he was a man at all — that haunted my nighttime hours was shrouded in black with eyes that glowed ominously through his hood. Always he pointed towards me, and always he moved closer with every dream. He was gaining on me, and there was nothing I could do to stop it.

"You get much sleep last night?" Leo asked me on our way to school.

"Not really," I replied, crossing Muldoon Ave on our way to the Epigosian School for Classical Studies in downtown Manhattan. The sun blazed bright on that warm September day. It was the second week of freshman year in high school, and as long as I could stay awake I was excited.

"You gotta do something about that. It's making you sluggish. " Leo said. He was right, and I knew it. For the past week, Ares, technically the god of war and our instructor in the arts of the sword and shield, had been on my case to improve my timing. I was getting my butt handed to me again and again in practice by Trinity Marks. She was one of my best friends but still…it was embarrassing.

Ordinarily, I wouldn't mind getting close to Trinity, even in battle, but it was getting uncomfortable being on the receiving end of sharp judo chops to the stomach so many times. My digestive system was not happy.

"TURNER, WATCH YOUR RIGHT SIDE!" Ares would yell out. "IF THIS WAS A REAL BATTLE, YOU'D BE DOWN IN HADES BY NOW!"

"I know, I know," I'd reply, jumping up quickly.

"If you know, then what's the problem?"

I stared at the grizzled god of war, trying to come up with an excuse that was manlier than having trouble sleeping. "I'll do better next time."

"You better!" Ares barked at me. "There is no place for sloppiness on the battle field." He scowled, the many scars on his face attesting to the truth behind his words.

The Epigosian School for Classical Studies appeared in the distance as we turned the corner. On the roof, men wearing yellow hard hats were pulling scaffolds down slowly. Construction of the fourth and final floor of Epigosian was nearing completion. Finally, we could set up the new skyscanner telescope Polytitus was talking so much about. Life on other planets is mathematically possible, he kept saying. I wonder what they did for fun on Neptune?

A ripple in the air high above us caught my attention. I stopped where I stood--the man from my nightmare was floating in midair!

"That's him!" I exclaimed.

"Who?" Leo said.

"The guy from my dreams…the dude in black—
Look!"

But it was too late. By the time Leo glanced over,
he had disappeared. "You sure there was someone there?"
He asked with a quizzical expression on his face.

"Positive…" I glanced once more in the direction of
the apparition. Empty.

"Dude, you need some shut eye," Leo remarked,
placing his hand on my shoulder.

"Forget it…let's just go in."

Two ornately decorated eagles on either side of the
entrance beckoned us forward. Inside, all along the first
floor walls were massive symbols of the Olympians: the
lightning bolt of Zeus; the trident of Poseidon; the graceful
Peacock of Hera. And on it went until every major
Olympian was represented. If you didn't know where you
were when you entered, you sure found out right away.

Appolonia, or as Athena called her, the raven
haired one, was walking towards us in the hallway. Leo
stared in her direction, pretty oblivious to my presence.

4

"Hi guys!" she exclaimed, flashing a smile in Leo's direction, her long, ebony colored hair flowing around her as if possessed of its own consciousness. She was a little shorter than Leo, with long nimble arms and eyes that radiated liveliness.

"Hi Appolonia," I replied. "Where you headed?"

"Bioengineering with Hephaestus."

"Booooorrrrrrring!" Leo exclaimed, chuckling in my direction. "He's like a gloomy mechanic."

"It's not that bad. Actually, I really like it," Appolonia replied. "He really shows how man and machine can combine in ways that benefit the earth. Have you heard of cyborgs?"

We stared at her in silence.

"Fascinating stuff!—paralyzed men being fused with smart machines that enable them to walk.

"Uhm, yeah," Leo quickly said. "I just meant that being the blacksmith to the gods must make him a boring teacher."

"Not at all. You should see his new armor designs for deep sea exploration. Coolest thing ever! Anyways, I have to go…don't want to miss lab. We're dissecting starfish in order to study its regenerative properties. Bye!" She darted off, full of enthusiasm for what lay ahead.

"That went well…" Leo said, watching Appolonia walk away.

"Real cool…" I commented.

"I know…totally made a fool of myself just then," he replied, a little downcast.

"Try and be yourself around her. It'll make it that much easier."

"Like you know?" He eyed me suspiciously.

'Trinity and I…it's complicated…I…"

He laughed and then put his arm around me, saying. "Don't sweat it bud. We'll figure it out together." I gave him a friendly shove.

"You don't have to fake it," I said. "Yesterday, you told me you wished you were in Hephaestus's class this semester."

"That's because Trinity told me Appolonia was in the class. But you're right, the technology he creates is mind blowing."

It was true. Historically known as the ugly and lame god because Hera, his mother, threw him off a cliff, Hephaestus was a genius with metal and machine. His capacity for invention was centuries ahead of what any major mortal scientist was working on currently. But that was because he was two thousand years older than any current mortal scientist.

Still, it was a privilege to see him work. Cassandra, the all-knowing artificial intelligence, was his invention. Housed in a satellite fifty miles above earth, you could access her from any computer like device: laptop, desktop, cellphone—even a car.

Hephaestus was the real deal, and we were lucky to have him as a teacher. In fact, striding through the halls of

Epigosian on the second week of school, I felt lucky to be there.

We headed towards first period class: Sustainable Agriculture with Demeter. "Samson! Leo! You're both late!" the goddess of the harvest exclaimed as we entered her class. She waved us towards two chairs in the front of the room. Fearsome and with a sparkle of good humor in her eyes, Demeter began the days lesson.

She snapped her fingers. A hologram of the earth materialized in the middle of the room.

"There is no reason people should go hungry on this planet," Demeter began. "America alone produces enough wheat to feed half the planet." A number of statistics flashed on the top of the hologram.

World agriculture produces 17 percent more calories per person today than it did 30 years ago, despite a 70 percent population increase. This is enough to provide everyone in the world with at least 2,720 kilocalories per person per day.

"Why is it, "Demeter asked, "that there is so much hunger in the world when the earth produces enough food to feed everyone?"

"Access, "Trinity replied.

"Correct!"

What followed was a discussion of how the world's resources were used. I sat there gazing at what seemed like an elderly woman with streaks in her hair the color of silver lightning. But Demeter was much more than that. No wonder Hades was afraid of her.

The Epigosian School had expanded since last year when Trinity, Leo and I were the only students there preparing for battle with Gideon Nefaris. Construction was almost completed, and Epigosian was growing both in size and student body. The halls were filled with new, eager faces. I wondered if they were like me and Trinity, descendants of super powered beings.

That's what Polytitus was explaining in his History of Genetic Mutations class.

"There is a noticeable change, "he began shortly after we walked into class, "in human genetics—mortals being born with *abnormal* abilities."

"How come it's not widely known...these powers?" asked Appolonia.

"The reason," Polytitus replied, "is that mankind considers these mutations as diseases, not adaptations." A picture of a man in India lying in a hospital bed completely covered in bandages. "This man," Polytitus explained, "is, we believe, a descendent of Apollo, the sun god.

"How do you figure?" Leo exclaimed. "He doesn't look so hot to me." Leo chuckled. "...get it...hot."

"We get it, Leo. Now will you please compose yourself." Polytitus stared severely at Leo, who slinked lower in his seat.

"This man," Polytitus continued, "has what the doctors call SHC. You might know of it as spontaneous human combustion or the ability to erupt into flames.

"You mean like the Human Torch from the Fantastic Four?" asked Jasmina Weatherley, one of the new students in the school. The red streaks in her hair gave the impression she herself was a descendent of Apollo.

"Well, we're not now talking about comic books, but, yes, essentially it is the same idea." Jasmina looked impressed, and so was I. Who knew Polytitus read comic books?

As the eternal guardian for the descendants of the many unions between Olympians and mortals, Polytitus was given the task to maintain the power immortal — Epios, the lineage that flowed from Olympian to mortal heroes.

Some of the greatest men and women of history were his students. Some, like Alexander the Great and George Washington lived up to his teachings and brought new possibilities to humanity. Others, like Genghis Khan and Hitler, turned their back on Polytitus and used the power for their own selfish desires, and almost brought the world to the brink of destruction.

One of these men was Gideon Nefaris, a man who would have stopped at nothing to possess the Orb of Orpheus, a mystical object that grants unlimited power.

We defeated him, and the Orb is now safeguarded in one of Hephaestus's super secure underground vaults.

"I heard you're having trouble sleeping," Trinity asked moments after we stepped out of class.

"Who told you that?" I asked, flashing an angry look at Leo.

"C'mon, dude!" he interjected. "You expect me not to tell Trinity about something like this, especially since we sit next to each other in Demeter's class. Agriculture is cool and everything, but you know I can't pay attention for that long."

"You're the one that should have told me," answered Trinity. She eyed me with a look as if to say, I thought we were friends.

"I know. I thought it would go away," I replied.

We headed to Planes of Reality with Hermes, a class that opened my eyes to what the messenger of the Olympians called alternate dimensions. It was wild, I know, but Hermes discussed it as being as much a reality as the Porsche I saw speeding down Muldoon avenue that morning.

We had a couple of minutes before class started, so I decided to tell Trinity everything.

"It seems to me," she said as we entered class a few minutes later, "that he's after something."

"What makes you say that?"

"He's getting closer to you with every nightmare...I'll explain afterwards." We sat down in the second row. Hermes, bald and smiling widely, entered the class seconds after. He was trim and tall, with skin the color of dark mahogany.

"Good morning. I hope everyone is well. Leo, sit up please." Leo sat straight up and folded his hands together. "Today we continue our study of inter-dimensional travel."

The lights dimmed and the board undulated and revealed three separate levels. "Here, you see three planes of reality: the top is where the immortals historically have called home: Mt. Olympus. Of course, strictly speaking, there is no actual Olympus. It is just a name that describes their plane of existence. The middle level you see here is earth, which includes the domain of Poseidon, the immortal of the oceans and seas, and that of Demeter, who holds sway over the harvest. Lastly," he pointed to the lowest level, one shrouded in dark mist, "we come to the dominion of Hades. All three of these planes exist simultaneously, and we are just now discovering that there may be many more."

My mind wandered as Hermes continued to explain the physics behind alternate dimensions. The light from the hologram cast an ominous glow around him.

Suddenly, the air shimmered. The feint outline of a shape materialized in the darkness.

Something was there.

Two bloodshot eyes became visible, then a hood, then an outstretched hand.

SAMSON TURNER! I AM COMING FOR YOU!

I jumped out of my seat.

The lights snapped on.

"Mr. Turner, is everything all right?" Hermes inquired. He turned towards the direction of my agitated gaze.

"No…I mean yes…just a little antsy…that's all."

A hand shot up in the air. It was Trinity saving me from an embarrassing situation.

"Yes, Ms. Marks."

"When you say planes of reality exist simultaneously, do you mean we all take up the same space?"

"Good question," replied Hermes sitting back on the top of the desk. "Yes, essentially that is correct. Einstein postulated that there might be hundreds of dimensions co-existing right next to one another. We are only aware of three. Of course, when I say we, I mean the Olympians. To the average mortal there is only one plane of existence." Another hand shot up. This time it was Appolonia.

"Ms. Byrnes."

"How do you travel from one dimension to another?"

"Another good question," stated Hermes. "There are ancient portals that have existed for centuries but they are few, and their locations have been lost through the years." Hermes glanced at me as if he was silently inquiring about something.

And then I got it. He was reminding me that I was one of those people that had accessed a portal in my trip to the underworld to bargain for the life of Polytitus.

"That's it!" I exclaimed suddenly, standing up. Everyone looked up at me as if I had three gorgons' heads.

"What is it, Mr. Turner?"

I looked around, immediately aware that I was talking to myself. "Uhh, nothing…just excited about the subject we're talking about." I shot a look at Trinity.

I finally understood what my nightmares were about.

"That's very nice," Hermes stated, looking a little irritated at my interruption. "Now, getting back to Appolonia's question. Inter-dimensional travel is much easier for us since Hephaestus invented the Portable Atom Collider, a machine the size of a cell phone that creates miniature black holes by smashing two atoms together with unequaled force. It allows us access to what Einstein called wormholes. If you turn to page 47 in *Relativity for Radicals* you'll see a diagram of one of these fascinating portals."

Thirty minutes later we walked out of class. "What was that all about?" asked Leo.

"I just realized something," I replied. "I think the guy in my dreams has to do with the trip I took to the underworld."

"Isn't that when you bargained with Hades?" Trinity asked.

"Yes."

"We need to go see Polytitus."

Chapter 2

Polytitus Explains

The office on the third floor of Epigosian was small and narrow from the outside. Its dark, oak paneled door bordered a frosted, glass panel on which read the following:

Genetic Mutations

Advisor to Heroes

Trinity knocked.

"Enter," a deep, gravelly voice called from within. We stepped into the room, amazed at what we just walked into. It was huge! Leo stuck his head outside just to make sure that we were in the same place.

What is it about Polytitus that always finds him in spaces that are so disproportionate? When we battled Gideon Nefaris, our headquarters was similar: tiny and plain on the outside, vast and high tech within.

He sat at a table facing the window, his back to us as he hunched over a large, dusty manuscript. Above his head a 60″ flat screen television displayed a map of the globe. Yellow dots blipped periodically throughout. To his right, several books piled up on one another like an asymmetrical miniature skyscraper. Farther ahead stood an oval wooden table with four chairs neatly surrounding it. On the wall were weapons of ancient times: Long swords bigger than Leo, crossbows that looked like you needed to be Hercules himself just to lift, and jeweled daggers that housed emeralds the size of golf balls. On the left hand wall was an immense map inlaid with squiggly dotted trails. In the center, in big black lettering read the word, *CORNUCOPIA.*

Trinity seemed transfixed as she approached the map. "Can it be?" she said as she followed one of the trails with her index finger all the way till it reached the middle.

"Where have you been hiding all this amazing stuff, Polytitus?" Leo exclaimed. Polytitus turned the page of his manuscript. A few moments later he closed the book and turned towards us.

"These are some of the possessions I've gathered in the eons I've been alive," he said with a warm smile on his face. That dagger there was given to me by Saladin, the mighty middle eastern ruler."

"Student of yours!" I inquired.

"You could say that," he replied mysteriously. He glanced over to where Trinity stood.

"Polyitus, is this map real?" she suddenly asked, still examining it closely.

"As real as the moon and the sky, young one."

"The Cornucopia exists?"

"Yes, in fact. We've just uncovered its approximate whereabouts using infrared scanning. That volume there on the table," he pointed to the book he was reading when we came in, "is now, for the first time, legible. It points to

20

somewhere in modern day Israel as the location of the Cornucopia."

"What's a corneycupia?" Leo interjected as he walked over to the map.

"The Cornucopia," Trinity corrected, "or the horn of abundance, is the horn that the infant Zeus wrenched from the goat, Amalthea. It was said to posses the ability to provide unending nourishment."

"You mean, unlimited food comes out of it?"

"That's right," Polytitus added.

"Wow!" Leo exclaimed in astonishment. "I need me one of those!"

Polytitus chuckled. "The young lion is always hungry I see." Young lion is what Polytitus calls Leo every now and then on account of his name. "I'm sure, however, you didn't come see me because Leo needs to eat...again."

"You're right, Polytitus. There's something more urgent, "Trinity said. "Tell him Samson."

I hesitated for a moment unsure of what I should say.

"Are you having nightmares?" Polytitus inquired.

"How did you know?" I asked, shocked that Polytitus was aware of my problem.

As if he had seen a ghost of someone long dead, his face dropped and a grim expression came over it. "I was afraid this would happen. Please," he pointed to the oval table, "let us sit down." We followed him and took our seats quietly. Even Leo knew better than to crack a joke. This was serious, and judging by the look on Polytitus's face I wasn't going to like what he was about to say.

"Do you remember being in the underworld last year, Samson?" he began.

"Of course. How could I forget?"

"Do you remember the bargain you made with Hades when you were down there?"

The memory of that faithful decision flashed across my mind.

You must give up a portion of your soul to

Hades, lord of the underworld.

Whatever it takes!

AGREED!

"Submerging you in the river Styx was the only thing that would save you. I had to do it," I explained. "And I'd do it again."

Polytitus managed a weak smile and said, "Thank you, dear boy. Your generosity shines through the ages." He stood up, stepped away from the table and walked over to the far end of the room. His hands behind his back, he stood there for some time meditating on what I thought was a situation that was going to go from bad to worse.

"The being haunting your dreams is Hades himself," he finally said. "He is coming for your soul."

"What!" Leo stood up in disbelief.

"Are you sure?" Trinity asked.

Polytitus turned and said, "It is a centuries old tradition that Hades stalks his victims in their sleep in order to prepare them for what is to come. If they be mortals, he so frightens them that when the time comes they willingly submit to the power of death in order to escape the unending mental anguish."

"And in Samson's case?" Trinity asked again.

"Samson's situation is similar to what happened with Persephone, the wife of Hades. It is only a portion of his soul that is at stake."

I recalled the story of Persephone, the daughter of Demeter, who was snatched by Hades and forced to be his queen down in the realm of the dead. Demeter, goddess of the harvest, scorched the earth until Zeus forced Hades to return her daughter. Wild with joy upon hearing that she was to be saved, Persephone accepted six pomegranate seeds from Hades, which, according to the law of the eternals, cemented her place in the underworld for six months of the year.

"I knew this was coming," I said. "I had a feeling Hades was going to take advantage of our bargain as soon as he could."

"You don't deal with the devourer of death without consequences," Polytitus stated, a look of worry upon his face. Suddenly, a knock on the door startled us. Without waiting for a greeting, a tall, beautiful woman with a pearl white complexion walked through the door.

It was Athena, goddess of wisdom and headmistress of Epigosian. "Polytitus, we need to talk about your recent research regarding the Cornucopia. Well hello there young ones." She looked at us gathered there at the table and then glanced at her watch. "Shouldn't you be in Strategies of Combat with Ares right about now?" It was true. We were playing hooky, and Ares wasn't going to like it.

"It seems headmistress that there is a matter urgent enough that we must attend to immediately," Polytitus explained. "Perhaps you should have a seat."

A half hour later, Athena knew the whole story. "Dear me, this is serious," she stated. "Hades is not someone with whom to trifle. I must think about our next step." She gazed at me and said, "That was a brave and foolish bargain you made, Samson Turner."

"I had no choice."

She smiled, and then said, "Meanwhile, schedules must be kept, and you all are very late to class."

"But what are we going to do?" Trinity demanded to know.

"There is only one thing to do," Athena replied. "We must go see Zeus."

Chapter 3

Eris, Goddess of Discord

trategies of Combat was a class for which I needed to prepare. Ares was a stickler for good form no matter what technique we were studying, which is why I usually practiced beforehand in preparation for the grilling I knew was coming my way.

The start of the year meant a review of previous methods. We were engaged in studying Capoeira, the Brazilian martial-art that evolved from dance and gymnastics. I loved learning how slaves developed this fighting technique in order to hide their purpose from their masters who only thought they were dancing.

On the door to the gymnasium was written a bunch of Greek words that I couldn't understand. Trinity, the brain, had to translate:

Ας κανένας άνθρωπ ος δεν Εισάγετε
π ου δεν π ιστεύει στη σιωπ ή του Ξίφους.

Let No Person Enter Who Does not

Believe in the Silence of the Sword

"Silence of the sword? What the heck is that?" Leo asked.

"Uhm…I think it means the ability of the sword as a weapon to silence opposition," I answered. "Ares mentioned it last year."

"But not just as a weapon, but as a symbol for defense," Trinity added. "I remember that class. Ares described the Athenians as having the belief that democracy and the ability to carry arms went together."

"Do you think it's still true today?" I asked.

"Ares will tell you yes, but I'm not sure."

The gymnasium was housed in the subterranean vault and encompassed the whole floor. Designed to hold at least two hundred students at full capacity, it was a massive space that housed enough equipment to train an army.

Ares did not play around.

I surveyed the area. To the far right, a number of students were practicing Tae Kwon Do—the Way of the Foot and the Hand. In the center was a boxing ring within which two others engaged in some intense sparring.

"Hold your hands up!" yelled a female voice. I looked over and saw a muscular woman standing on the outskirts of the ring. She spotted me, flashed an angry look and returned to the fight in front of her. Her arms bulged out of a black t-shirt with a picture of a skull and bones and the heading COME AND GET IT! displayed on top. For a moment I thought it was Ares, so much did she look like him.

"Oh no!" Trinity exclaimed.

"What's wrong?" I asked.

"We've got trouble," she replied looking over to where the she-man stood. "That's Eris."

29

"Who's Eris?"

"The goddess of Discord," Leo replied. "Sister to the god of war." I turned to Leo, impressed with his knowledge. "I pay attention in History class. You should try it sometimes."

"So what's the big deal," I said, after giving Leo a playful shove.

"Eris would ride out with her brother during his war mongering days and sow anger and confusion on the battlefield."

"She's Hera's favorite," Trinity continued, "and her presence here could mean only one thing."

"What's that?"

"YOU ARE LATE!" Ares bellowed, stomping towards us from a group who were doing push ups.

"We were with Polytitus," I explained.

"THAT IS NO EXCUSE!" A vein popped out of the war god's forehead. "GIVE ME FIVE LAPS AROUND THE GYM!"

"Can I change first?"

"MOVE IT!"

We dashed into the locker rooms.

"I hate these uniforms," Leo quipped.

"They're not so bad," I replied, pulling my t-shirt over my head.

"Easy for you say. You have the sign of Zeus on your shirt. Look at me...empty."

It was true. For some strange reason, Epigosian gym uniforms signified your place in the Olympic pantheon. There was an empty space in the middle of Leo's shirt. "Athena said she would figure out something soon," I offered, trying to make him feel better. "She can't just make up an Olympian."

"Whatever...just because I don't have an immortal as a descendent doesn't mean I should be a second class citizen."

"Now you're exaggerating. Everybody loves you here. C'mon let's go — Ares will have our head if we don't get out there soon.

We sprinted out and began running immediately. All the while Eris eyed me suspiciously. She walked over to her brother and whispered in his ear. The god of war shook his head furiously. She insisted. He looked our way, a worried expression on his face.

"TURNER, "he shouted. "GET OVER HERE!" I ran over, unsure of what to expect.

"What now!" I groaned, irritated by the unpleasantness I knew was coming my way.

"It's time for you to train," he explained.

"I thought that's what I was doing."

"Never mind that. I want you to meet Eris, goddess of Discord and my — "

"Sister, yes, I've heard all about it.," I explained.

"Why…what have you heard?" Ares was suddenly upset. "She is not here to take my place, if that's what you think! Hera does not control me! She may be my mother but she is not my master."

"Brother, dear," Eris interjected. Her voice slithered out of her. "I am sure the famous Samson Turner has no clue to what you are saying." She extended her hand. "Greetings, it is good to finally meet you."

With some hesitation, I reciprocated. A flash of intense pain shot through my arm as she squeezed my fingers almost to the point of breaking.

I pulled my hand free. Whatever her motive, Eris definitely made her feelings about me crystal clear.

Trinity spied the interaction and rushed over. "So this is Trinity Marks," Eris quipped. "I've heard much about you."

"The daughter of Hera flatters me," Trinity replied and took a slight bow.

"Manners and good looks. Brother dear, you sure have kept these delightful children to yourself," Eris half whispered playfully in his ear. Ares grunted and glanced from Eris to us and back again. Something was coming, that much his face made clear.

How weird, I thought, that this muscle bound Olympian was acting like the most prim and proper of women.

"Shall we commence with the trials," Eris inquired.

"What trials?" Leo asked, sidling alongside me. "You never said anything about any trials, Ares."

"It is Hera's doing," Ares explained. "She asked that Eris be given the authority to judge the quality of our training."

"Does Athena know about this?" Trinity asked.

"This comes straight from Hera, the queen of the Olympians. Athena has no authority over me," Eris snarled as she turned towards the boxing ring. With one massive leap up, she jumped into it with a big thud.

"Turner, you're up, "Ares ordered. "Good luck," he said, half heartedly patting me on the back.

Judging from the way Eris was cracking her knuckles, I was going to need it. I stepped towards my opponent, but Trinity stopped me.

"Let me take care of this," she offered. "We girls know how to handle one another." With a running jump, she somersaulted into the ring and landed steps away from a very surprised goddess of discord. "I hope I'll be worthy enough of your skills," she said to Eris.

Astonishment at Trinity's boldness turned to fury as Eris set her sights on her young opponent. A hush fell over the gymnasium as the students stopped their activities and encircled the ring. Within, Trinity and Eris prepared to tangle.

The goddess of discord lunged at Trinity first, grabbing on to her shoulders in what looked like a Greco-Roman wrestling take down. Using both her legs, Trinity swiftly fell onto her back and hurled Eris across the ring. In a flash the Olympian was up and charging Trinity, who was about to round house kick Eris in the neck. But this time, she was ready, and grabbed Trinity's foot before it made contact.

With a violent motion, Eris swung Trinity's foot around her until she was brought down to the floor. Still holding on to Trinity's leg, Eris came down on it with the full weight of her body.

The sound of a loud crack filled the silent room. Trinity lay on the floor whimpering in pain.

I rushed over to help her. Leaping into the ring I smashed Eris in the face with my knee. She tumbled headlong into the far corner. I needed to get her away from Trinity before she did anymore damage.

"Samson Turner coming to the rescue of his girlfriend...how cute," Eris snarled in mockery. "Well, too bad because nothing is going to help you and your friends now that Hera is in charge." She let out a blood curdling scream and charged at me.

"Not this time!" Leo exclaimed as he leaped into the fight. Acting as a wall between Eris and me and Trinity, he seemed to dare the goddess of discord to take one step further.

"Mortal, do you really think you can stop me?" she snarled.

"I'm sure as heck going to try, "Leo replied, circling Eris.

"ENOUGH! WHAT IS THE MEANING OF THIS?"

It was Athena.

"Hera requested that Eris be present during training, headmistress, "explained Ares, scuttling over like he was in trouble.

"And you didn't tell me about this? You didn't clear it with me?"

Ares was silent. Athena was about to blow. "I shall deal with you later, brother. Leo, take Trinity to the infirmary now." Leo gently picked Trinity up and carried her away. "Samson, come with me." I quickly sidled over to Athena.

"Where are we going? " I asked.

"You have an important appointment," she said as we headed out of the gymnasium.

Chapter 4

A Wormhole to Olympus

It wasn't until we were speeding along through the wormhole that I realized we were no longer on Earth. Outside the gymnasium, Athena had pulled out what looked like a souped up IPhone.

"Are you ready for this? "she asked.

"Ready for what?" I asked in disbelief. "You haven't told me where we're headed."

"To see Zeus, of course." She punched a button and suddenly a tiny black dot appeared before us. Slowly it widened until, by degrees, it was large enough to admit a full sized human being.

"Is this safe?" I asked, taking a step back away from what looked like a miniature black hole.

"From all preliminary tests we've done on what Hephaestus calls the Portable Atom Collider, its safety is at 85%.

"What about the other 15%?"

"Well, it seems the Heisenberg Principle does hold true in certain cases."

"What does that mean?"

"Well...sometimes ears end up as noses, but that's quickly corrected on the other end. You ready?"

She stepped into the wormhole. Despite my worries about toes ending up on my head, I followed her.

If you've ever put your hand under a vacuum cleaner and felt the power of its suction, multiply that a million times and you have an idea as to what it's like to travel through a worm hole. It was as if my body was being stretched thinner and thinner. The weird thing is I didn't feel any pain.

And then, suddenly, we arrived at our destination with a loud pop. It was so bright I had to shield my eyes.

Soon enough, what I saw was barely recognizable.

I had seen Zeus only one previous time. It was in a library where he was reading. White haired with a beard like Abraham Lincoln's, and wearing a tie with a large sun on it, I remember him radiating warmth and wisdom.

But the being who sat on an immense stone throne in front of me was nothing like the one I saw that day in the room filled to the brim with books. Here was a gigantic man, the size of whose body was at least fifteen feet high. Sitting there, he stroked a white beard that ran down to his chest. In his other hand he held an enormous metal lightning bolt. To his right sat a young woman whose face I immediately recognized.

Athena.

Encased in flowing white robes with a wreath upon her head, she too was enormous. To the right and left of both immortals were massive stone thrones which were presently empty.

The smell of ammonia hung heavy in the air. Just above me, thick billowy clouds slowly roamed.

"Where am I?" I asked the two giants.

"Be at ease, Samson Turner, for you are in Olympus, the home of the Immortals," Athena declared in a voice that boomed like a megaphone.

"Why do you look like that?"

"My earthly form is one I take out of necessity, as my true frame would certainly frighten mortals."

"I see what you're saying," I quipped, looking from Athena to Zeus and back to Athena again. They certainly were big... and a little scary.

"My daughter has informed me of your bargain with the lord of the underworld, Samson Turner," Zeus began, his voice so deep it sounded like the rumbling of an earthquake.

"It couldn't be helped. I had to save Polytitus," I replied defiantly.

"Rest assured, young hero, that it was a most valiant deed," Zeus answered. A half smile curved his lips.

41

"The dilemma we face now is that of reclaiming your soul." Athena turned and whispered into Zeus's ear.

He thought about what she said for a moment and then remarked, "There is another way."

"The bargain I made with Hades was done in good faith. Polytitus lives," I interjected. "I'm not ready to back out on our agreement, not even if it means spending time down in the underworld."

"That may be true, Samson, but it was not in the dark lord's power to make that deal. Since the kidnapping of Persephone eons ago, Demeter, her mother, has lobbied the Olympians to create a law barring all underage agreements."

Behind Zeus a large parchment appeared suspended in mid-air. From top to bottom was a list itemized by what I recognized to be Roman Numerals. Everything else looked like it was written in a foreign language.

"Father," Athena explained, "the boy can not yet read Greek."

"Can't read Greek?! What are you teaching them down there in that school of yours?"

Zeus snapped his fingers, and immediately one of the sentences on the parchment transformed into English.

Minors cannot be bargained with in matters of death and love.

"While Hades was forbidden to contract with you according to the Eternal Laws," Zeus explained, "by making that deal for the life of Polytitus, you have, nevertheless, opened the door to death's claim. But we shall see what can be done about that."

Suddenly, Zeus held up his lightning bolt over his head and exclaimed, "BY THE POWER ETERNAL, I SUMMON HADES, LORD OF THE UNDERWORLD, TO THE HALLS OF OLYMPUS!"

A flash erupted some distance from where I stood. Dense smoke cascaded around what looked like a man about the size of Athena.

"I HATE WHEN YOU DO THAT, BROTHER!" declared a voice thick with suppressed anger. The smoke dissipated, and I immediately realized who stood towering above me—it was the man from my nightmares! Pale white with smooth black hair, his eyes glowed red.

"Hades, this is a vital matter. Your presence here is necessary," Zeus exclaimed.

"It is not enough that you relegated me to the depths of the dark realms, while you and Poseidon carved up the richest areas for yourselves, but to insult me even further you summon me at will like a mere slave!" Hades trembled with rage as he stepped closer to Zeus.

"Please hear us, Uncle," Athena interjected. "This is a matter of souls and salvation."

"WHAT OF IT! YOU HAVE NO RIGHT TO QUESTION ME ON SUCH MATTERS!" Hades turned around like a caged dog searching for something towards which he could vent his fury. He spotted me suddenly.

Slowly he stood up. "I see now what this is all about," he hissed.

"You, I'm sure, are quite aware that you can not bargain with minors," Zeus stated, banging his bolt on the floor.

A look of stony determination fell upon Hades. "I saw an opportunity and I took it," he said.

"Yes, that often seems to be the case," Zeus sneered. "Nevertheless, since the law is very clear on this matter, the agreement is no longer valid."

"I know the law quite well, brother! Do not presume to lecture me! I am aware the hero must accept the quest in order to reclaim his soul!" Hades flashed a furious look at me.

"I won't refuse anything put my way!" I interrupted. "I'm not afraid!"

"But you will be mortal...you will be."

Hades turned towards Zeus and said, "And what about you, brother dear? Will you agree to any quest?"

"Any you put in front of the heir of Hercules!" Zeus exclaimed.

"By the laws?"""

"FATHER DON'T!" Athena cried out. But it was in vain.

Raising his crackling lightning bolt above his head, he brought it down with force and declared, "BY THE LAWS OF TARTARUS!"

Athena stood up slowly. I searched her face for some understanding of what had just happened. A smile, crafty and malicious, crept over the face of Hades. Zeus sat back in his throne with an air of confidence.

Hades looked from Zeus to his daughter and back again. It was clear the god of death had something on his mind.

"I want the Amulet of Immortality!"

"What!" Zeus uttered in shock.

"You are insane! It cannot be done!" Athena declared.

"It will—Zeus has sworn on it!" Hades hissed.

"You would risk the demise of the Olympians—your brethren—for the soul of a mortal?" Zeus declared. "If The Amulet of Immortality was taken out of its casing, it would mean the end of life as we know it for the Olympians. We would cease to exist. Why would you risk all that?"

"HAHAHAHAHAHAHAHA! It was my *brethren* who laughed behind my back and called me the gloomy king! It was my *brothers* who sent me to the underworld into the arms of sweet death! It is she who I serve now!"

"Be sensible, uncle," Athena pleaded. "You have nothing to gain here!"

"HAHAHAHAHAHAHAHA! You are as foolish as your father, goddess of wisdom. I stand to gain the greatest prize of all—the souls of the Olympians!"

Hades turned and pointed a gnarled finger at me. "By the unbreakable laws of Tartarus, you will bring me the Amulet of Immortality! Fail and I will claim your soul for eternity!"

An sudden explosion sent me reeling back ten feet. Soon enough, I struggled up, trying to clear my head.

Hades was gone. I searched the faces of the downcast Olympians for a better understating of what had just happened.

What was the Amulet of Immortality? What did it have to do with the end of Olympus?

Zeus held his head in his hands. Finally, Athena stood up and said, "Samson Turner, by the eternal laws you have been given a quest you cannot refuse. It is a most treacherous journey. May the ancients guide your way!"

Chapter 5

Cyclops Everywhere

Great, I thought. I'm about to go on a quest even Athena describes as dangerous and I don't even know what it is.

But I didn't have time to think about it much. Within a flash, I was transported to another place.

All around me flew young fairy like girls in wing tipped sandals. They flittered across beds, tending to the sick who were placed next to one another in neat rows. I spotted a familiar face with her leg up.

Trinity waved me over. Leo and Appolonia were sitting by her bedside.

"Where have you been, stranger?" Trinity asked as I clasped her hand. Leo wrapped his arm around my shoulder. With a mischievous wink, he gestured towards one of the fairies. I elbowed him.

It was good to see friendly faces.

"Talking to Zeus," I answered.

"What! *The* Zeus! Like, king of the Olympians, Zeus!" Leo asked in astonishment.

"That's right." a voice from behind me interjected.

It was Hermes. He sauntered towards us with a clipboard in his hand.

"Samson has been given a mission." He motioned one of the fairies over and handed her the clipboard. She, in turn, gave him a small brown paper packet. Feline eyes and a diminutive shaped head gave her the look of a being from a planet inhabited by humanoid cats.

"Aren't you Samson Turner?" the fairy nurse asked, hovering beside me. Her skin was the color of porcelain. Blue-green hair flowed all around her face.

"Um, yes, that's me," I replied. Leo flashed me a grin.

"We've heard all about you here in the infirmary," she said, inching closer to me.

"Samson is busy now," Trinity interjected, an irritated look on her face.

"Yeah, why don't you do your job and take care of that boy over there. He looks like he needs help...isn't that pus oozing out of his arm?" Appolonia chimed in, strands of her thick, ebony colored hair standing on end.

How does her hair do that, I thought?

The fairy nurse flashed an annoyed look at Appolonia, and then darted away to tend to someone who had a strange green colored liquid coming out of his nose.

"Don't you just love Naiads?" Appolonia quipped. "Always interested in the boys."

"Not this boy!" Trinity exclaimed. We all looked at her in surprise. "Uhm, what I meant was that they really should focus on the work of nursing the sick students of Epigosian."

Blood rushed into my cheeks.

"Riiiiiight, "Leo replied. "Those Naiads are so irresponsible."

"Stuff it Leo," Trinity said, averting my gaze. "I'll handle the Naiads, thank you very much."

Naiads were spirits of the lakes and springs. I recalled a lesson Polytitus gave on the many ancient life forms that inhabited the waters around us. Naiads were jealous creatures who were known to lull young boys to sleep in order to drag them into the water.

Note to self — don't mess with a Naiad!

"All right now, settle down." Hermes said. "Let's focus on Trinity please. She's the one that needs our attention now." Unraveling the brown packet, Hermes revealed white powder that looked a bit like finely crushed chalk. With just a pinch, he sprinkled it on Trinity's fractured leg.

"Hermes, I didn't know you carry fairy dust with you?" Leo chortled.

"That my friend is no fairy dust, "Hermes explained. "The extracellular matrix is the source of the

Olympian's immortality." Hermes directed his gaze my way. "…and the object of the quest Samson is to go on."

"I thought it was an amulet that Hades wants," I said.

"The Amulet is housed in stone far below the earth. Through it runs water that is the source of our long life. Somehow the amulet changes the water — imbues it with a property that speeds up the regeneration within a body."

"You mean to tell me, " I interjected, "that the Olympians are mortal?"

"Not exactly, "Hermes corrected. "We are an ancient race, on earth long before humans evolved into their present state. But the amulet goes even further back than the Olympians, and it is just now that we've learned the science behind it. For as long as I can remember, the water that sustains the Nectar and Ambrosia upon which we feed originated from one source. From the first touch upon our lips, we realized that this water was magical, and that it was the key to immortality. Only recently have we discovered that within its molecular structure is a matrix that speeds up cell regeneration. "

"I can't believe it!" Trinity exclaimed. Suddenly, she sat upright. A second later, she flung the splint off her leg and jumped off the bed.

"No way!" I exclaimed. The Naiads all turned towards my direction. "Five minutes ago, you could barely move your leg."

"I know," she replied doing a front somersault across the floor of the infirmary. "Woohooo!!"

"Just in time," Leo exclaimed. "Lenny's pizzeria is calling our name. Appolonia, you wanna come?"

"Sure," she replied. Leo grabbed his backpack and they ran out. Trinity and I waved goodbye to Hermes and followed.

Dusk beckoned the evening moon forward as my stomach informed me it was dinnertime. Lenny's Pizzeria stood two blocks away from Epigosian, its big neon sign a familiar site to us on the way home from school.

The savory aroma of pizza wafted through the air as we walked in. The place was packed with people grabbing a bite to eat.

"What'll ya have," Lenny asked, smiling at us broadly, his big belly and chef's hat creating the illusion of an Italian Santa Claus. "Wait, don't tell me, Leo — pineapples."

"You know me well, Len. And don't forget the fruit punch…please."

"Pepperoni, please…and a water. "Trinity requested.

"Samson…olives?"

"Yup and a fruit punch as well, please," I replied.

"And what about you, little lady," Lenny asked Appolonia.

"Pineapples, huh…I think I'll try that out." She smiled at Leo.

We paid and headed to the back of the restaurant. "Right here, "Leo called out, walking towards an empty table. A picture of a gondola floating down a Venetian canal stood on the wall behind us.

We were so hungry that the only sound that could be heard was chewing. Appolonia finally broke the silence. "A quest, huh…that must be so cool. I'm always reading about them. That one with Perseus and Medusa rocked."

"It's something I have to do." I took a swig of my fruit punch and debated the merits of filling in the background details for Appolonia. Before I could make up my mind, Leo did it instead.

"Hades is coming for Samson."

"Thanks Leo…real comforting," Trinity interjected.

"What? — it's the truth. No sense beating around the bush."

"Wow! Hades…really?!" Appolonia exclaimed. "I've wanted to get a look at him. Is he like super scary?"

"Kind of, in a crazy clown sort of way," I answered.

"Wow…are you frightened?"

"Yeah…sort of…but I have to do it."

"We have to do it, Samson," Trinity corrected. "You are not alone. We're going to do this together."

"That's right, "Leo exclaimed.

"Count me in too!" Appolonia chimed in eagerly. "I would love to help!"

"You hear that, Samson?" Leo nudged me playfully. "Appolonia's on board as well!"

I felt a rush of gratitude for my friends. I wasn't alone, and that meant all the difference in the world.

"Is it true you're a descendent of Athena?" Trinity suddenly asked Appolonia.

"That's what Hermes told me, but Athena has never spoken to me. I think it's because she can't claim any descendants."

"Why?" Leo asked.

"According to the mythology, she was born from the head of Zeus. Supposedly she took a vow of chastity…but I don't know how long that held up." Appolonia's eyes twinkled with mischief.

Leo chortled, and a stream of fruit punch flew across the table, dousing us in red juice. As gross as it was, we all erupted in laughter as Leo wiped the red stuff from his face.

It was early evening before we realized how much time had gone by. We stepped out into the early fall night. A powerful gust of wind suddenly blew past us. Trinity grabbed my hand for support. Something like an electric shock quickly run through my body. She smiled at me and I felt, somehow, that things would work out.

Leo wanted to take a detour down Mulberry street, through an alleyway behind Trattoria Romana, the Italian restaurant that served the best Spaghetti Bolognese in all of New York city. Even when you weren't hungry, you couldn't beat the smell. What can I say, Leo always thinks with his stomach.

"You sure this is the right way?" Trinity asked as we headed down the dimly lit passageway. A light flickered in the distance on, casting ghoulish shadows on the graffiti streaked walls.

"Positive," Leo replied. "It's just up ahead." He led the way, followed by Appolonia and Trinity. I brought up the rear. It was eerily quiet save for the sound of water dripping from the roof of the building to our right.

Something about it didn't feel right, I thought. Suddenly, the sound of steps made us stop dead in our tracks.

"Samson, did you hear that?" Trinity asked.

"Sure did," I answered, turning around slowly to get a glimpse of what lay behind us.

From the shadows emerged a face I had only recently come to know. The skull and bones on her t-shirt was unmistakable.

It was Eris, the goddess of discord. She didn't look happy to see us. Behind her stood three hulking beings, their faces partly masked by the dark.

"What do you want, Eris?" I demanded

"What I want is simple, Samson Turner — I WANT YOU!" She stepped forward and so did her bodyguards. It was then I realized who it was she brought with her.

"Cyclops!" Trinity gasped.

There they stood — three one eyed giants gnashing their pointy teeth as if they hadn't eaten in months. Hairy with arms the size of tree trunks, they kept pounding their fists into their palms. *Tales of Mythical Creatures* by Flavius the Wise did not do justice to the monsters that looked ready to eat my friends and me.

"Oh boy…," Leo said. He turned to Appolonia and asked, "Are you ready for this?"

"I hope so," she replied, stepping behind him.

Within a flash, Keravnos, my trusted sword, appeared in my hand. There was no way I was going to let Eris and her one eyed goons hurt my friends. If she wanted a fight, she was about to get one.

"AAAAAAHHHHHHH!!!!" A Cyclops with a tattoo of a heart on his bicep charged at me, yelling, "YOU DIE NOW!"

Thick gobs of drool dribbled from his gaping mouth. I sprinted at him and, before he knew what was happening, swept his legs from under him. Quickly, I hit him on the head with my sword's handle. He crumpled to the floor unconscious.

"BROTHER!" Another Cyclops with shaggy hair and what looked to me like three gold teeth, turned towards me. He pointed his thick finger and said, "ME BREAK YOUR BONES!"

With long, powerful strides he bolted towards me. I clutched Keravnos tightly with both hands ready to do battle with my one-eyed foe.

But I didn't have a chance. Leo came flying from the corner with a round house kick aimed at the big goon's head. This Cyclops though was faster than his brother. He grabbed Leo's leg, swung him around and threw him against the wall.

"LEO!" Appolonia screamed. She ran over to where he lay slumped on the floor.

It was no use. He was out cold.

Trinity was battling Eris in close hand to hand combat. She was holding her own against the Olympian, but I could see Eris was getting too many shots.

Two Cyclops, one shorter and more muscular than the other, walked slowly in my direction. They mumbled something to each other and then proceeded to encircle me. Trinity had her hands full and Leo was unconscious.

It was me against them.

Or so I thought until Appolonia ran into the fight. It must've been the pain inflicted on Leo that transformed her because the Appolonia I saw that day was nothing like I'd seen before.

Ebony colored hair stood on end all around her head. Her eyes glowed like big oncoming headlights. It suddenly occurred to me that there was more to Appolonia than we knew about.

Slowly but with deadly intent, she stepped towards the surprised Cyclops. The shorter one lunged at her. Almost as if it had a mind of its own, a thick strand of Appolonia's hair shot out, wound around the Cyclops leg, and dangled him in mid air. "HELP ME, BROTHER!" he screamed. 'THE WITCH HAS ME!"

Holding Keravnos up high, I rushed at the taller Cyclops.

But it was too much for him. Swiftly, he picked up his dazed brother and staggered away.

"You forgot someone!" Appolonia yelled as she swung her prisoner towards his brothers. They tumbled forward like pins being hit by a bowling ball. Beaten and dazed, they picked themselves up and scurried away mumbling something about human magic.

Her cronies gone, Eris seemed less confident about her position. Trinity kept raining blows upon her head until finally it looked like the Olympian would give out.

I ran over to help.

"It's over!" I yelled.

"I will be back, Samson Turner! You can depend on it!" she sneered, and then, a second later, disappeared into the shadows.

"Are you ok?" I asked Trinity.

She nodded as she knelt down on the floor in exhaustion.

We ran over to Leo to check out his condition. Dazed, he stood up with some help. "Did we win?"

"You could say that," I replied.

"I think we did all right, " Trinity surmised, flashing a grin at Appolonia.

"That may be true now," I replied. "But there's something brewing and it's big."

Chapter 6

Robots to the Rescue

"Samson, wake up! You're going to be late for school!"

"Samson, did you hear me? It's late!"

"I'm up! I'm up!"

Mornings were tough for me, especially after fighting one-eyed monsters. I stumbled out of bed and pulled the shades open. The bright October sun streamed through the window.

"Did you clean up?" my mom called out from the dining room.

"I can't do everything at once! " I called back, annoyed at the prospect of having to wake with so many

65

questions. My room was fine, I thought, surveying the space. Socks on the floor didn't constitute a mess.

I dressed quickly and headed downstairs, but just as I took that first step onto the staircase, I stopped. Dang, my mom sure knows how to get inside my head. I rushed back, grabbed the socks and did a jump shot into the hamper before quickly heading down.

"I have to talk to you," I said to my mother as she placed a bowl of fruit loops in front of me.

Susan Turner, my mom, was one tough woman. Losing my father when I was just a baby made her very cautious in the world. So you can imagine how she felt when she found out I was a descendent of Hercules. I hated that I had to worry her further, but I had to talk about what was going on.

She sat down and sipped from a cup of coffee, her long brown hair tied into a bun that perched neatly on top of her head. She looked like a kind but stern teacher. "I'm listening."

I told her about my nightmares and the deal I made with Hades. Her face dropped. She placed the coffee cup slowly on the kitchen table. For a long moment she said nothing.

"You should have told me," she finally said.

"I know...I didn't want to worry you."

"Hades...couldn't you have made a deal with Apollo or even Aphrodite?"

I chuckled. Mom smiled a little.

"I need to go on a quest," I continued. "It's the only way to regain my soul."

She stood up, refilled her coffee cup and turned to face me. "I'm starting to get worried."

"Don't. I've got Leo and Trinity with me, and a new girl named Appolonia who can do amazing things with her hair," I replied. "Plus, Zeus and Athena are watching over us." I got up and gave her a hug. "I'll be ok...I promise." She squeezed me tight.

"I know you have to do this but...be careful."

"I will…thanks mom." I turned towards the door.

"Samson."

"Yeah?"

"Your father would be proud." I ran and hugged her once more. Ten minutes later I was on my way to school.

Athena was waiting for me at the entrance. "Samson, please come with me."

"Where are we going?"

"To see Hephaestus about getting you the right equipment for your quest."

We stepped into Epigosian and headed towards the first floor elevator. Athena pressed a triangular button, and we plummeted down.

When the elevator stopped, my stomach was in serious need of some stability. It felt like I had just done ten loop the loops on a roller coaster.

The elevator doors swung open. I took a second to look around: metallic grey machines crowded the room. The rhythmic sound of metal striking metal filled my ears.

On the walls were tools that seemed strangely familiar: a two foot screwdriver with spikes all along its shaft; pliers the size of a small bicycle, and bolts that resembled tires you find on mid-sized trucks. A veil of smoke filled up the room. I took a couple of steps forward to get a better look at my surroundings.

Suddenly, a human shape became discernible. "Whose there?" I called, startled by the form a few steps ahead of me.

"No one…well, at least not people." Athena replied. "Look carefully." Athena clapped her hands, dissipating the smoke that obscured my vision.

They were robots! — all manner of sizes!

I reached out for one that looked like a WWF wrestler with glasses.

"DON'T TOUCH THAT!" a deep, gravelly voice called out from the far end of the room. I turned and saw a man the size of a small tree holding an immense hammer across his right shoulder. Arms the size of baby alligators with a face the color of bronze, his eyes flashed red as he walked towards me. "Janus is alert," he warned.

Whatever that meant I had a feeling I didn't want to find out.

"How are you, sister?" the man asked Athena.

I realized then that I was standing in front of Hephaestus, the blacksmith and inventor to the Olympians. "I'm well, brother. Thank you," Athena replied, extending her hand. Hephaestus shook it warmly.

The elevator swung open again. Out ran Trinity, eager eyed and with a smile on her face. "I'm sorry to intrude headmistress," Trinity blurted. "But I had to come. Samson isn't going on the quest alone."

"That's quite all right, Ms. Marks. I thought you'd be joining us eventually." I flashed Trinity a grateful smile.

"Now that we're all here, sister, " Hephaestus interrupted. "Can you tell me the reason for all these visitors?" In the background, I heard the sound of machines grinding to a halt.

I glanced around the room—was he controlling these machines?

"We are here, brother, because young Samson is going on a quest to retrieve the Amulet of Immortality."

"You don't say?" The god of all things metal and machine looked me over. "Hades involved?" Athena nodded. "Of course he is. He's been after that amulet ever since he was relegated to the underworld. That has always been his plan."

He turned and headed towards the back of the room where a massive computer screen flashed blue and yellow lights. "So, what will you be needing from me?" Hephaestus inquired. Janus the robot raised its head, and silently lumbered after his master.

"We need to outfit Samson with the necessary tools to retrieve the amulet," Athena explained. "And we need to do this immediately. He only has one month."

"WHAT!?" Trinity and I blurted out. "A month! How can I do this in such a short time?" I asked.

"You're going to have to," Athena explained. "And Hephaestus is going to help you."

"Humph! Hephaestus is always helping others...when will others help Hephaestus." The burly Olympian pressed a couple of buttons on the keyboard in front of him. A few moments later I heard a voice that was instantly recognizable.

"Hephaestus, Janus is still in development. He may not be ready for service."

It was Cassandra! We hadn't seen each other since the battle with Gideon Nefaris.

"Never mind that, Cassandra. He is ready for the field. I have checked the systems."

"That may be so," Cassandra explained, "but his artificial intelligence is not yet up to the age we envisioned. As he is now, he has the emotional capacity of a thirteen year old."

Hephaestus glanced at me and Trinity. "That sounds about right. At any rate, he'll just have to learn as he goes."

Standing a few steps away from us, Janus the robot seemed not to take notice of the conversation between Cassandra and her maker. Covered in gleaming metal the color of silver, his face looked strangely similar to that of Hephaestus, except for the thick horn rimmed glasses perched on his iron nose.

Glasses on a robot—that was a new one.

But he wasn't just a robot. Something about him looked human, even childlike. I had an urge to ask him if he wanted to play a game of basketball.

"Greetings, Samson and Trinity. I thought it was your brainwaves I was detecting," Cassandra said.

"Hi Cassandra. It's good to see...er...hear you." Trinity replied.

"It seems your brainwave indicator is working well, Cassandra," Hephaestus grumbled. "Goes to show I know what I'm doing."

"I do not question your ability, lord of blacksmiths and artists," Cassandra explained. "Just your haste in exposing Janus to situations for which he might not be prepared." Hephaestus grunted and turned to Janus with tools in hand.

As if by a silent, mental command, Janus lifted his arm and a flap on his back slid open. The robot's head fell upon his chest. Hephaestus tinkered with Janus's circuitry for the next few minutes. Finally, with a last twist, the back panel closed and Janus's eyes came back to life.

"Samson, please step forward," Hephaestus ordered. I stepped closer to Janus, who turned to face me almost as if he sensed my approach. "Meet Janus. He will accompany you on your quest."

Suddenly, a voice with a youthful, English accent came out of the hulking robot. "Hello, Samson Turner. Good to meet you."

"Hello," I replied. It seemed awkward talking to a robot at first. A hundred questions ran through my mind: How did he function? Did he actually think?

"My Neutron Cortex processes information, if that's what you mean by *thinking*."

Wait—Did Janus just read my mind? "How did you get inside my head?" I blurted out.

"I am attuned to your particular brain waves, and can interpret the activity of your mind. You can request anything of me with a mere thought."

I glanced at Trinity. She smiled. We were both thinking the same thing:

Any request with just a thought…

"Processing…The way to win Space Odyssey Adventure is to mine the comets for hidden gold," Janus explained. "Sounds like a cool game, Samson."

"Samson, Janus is an advanced robotics unit," Athena reprimanded. "He is not to be used for winning video games."

"Sorry…I couldn't help it," I replied. Trinity chortled. Having Janus around was going to be one sweet experience. Yet in the back of my mind, I had a nagging feeling that access to my thoughts 24/7 was not the best idea.

"If you are not comfortable with that function," Janus replied as if in conversation with my mind. "I will turn it off till you ask once more."

"Please do, " I answered.

Whatever lay in front of me — Hades, Eris, the goddess of Discord, somehow Janus being there made me feel a whole lot more confident.

'That's all he'll need," Hephaestus declared. "Janus is equipped with a ten petabyte processor powered by a miniature fusion reactor. He is as high tech as it gets." Folding his arms on his chest, he looked over his creation like a father beaming proudly at his son's first homerun.

"Very well," Athena remarked. "There is no time to waste. You leave tonight."

Chapter 7

The Map of Mephistopheles

Athena spoke to us for the final time in her office. Shelves of thick, leather bound books lined the walls like thoughtful sentries waiting to be called out. A large white spotted owl perched itself on top of a porcelain bust of a serious looking man with a long white beard.

"Erasmus, "Athena called out, "please don't sit on Socrates. You know he doesn't like it." Erasmus let out a loud hoot and proceeded to remain exactly where he was before. The goddess of wisdom stared at the defiant, green eyed owl, obviously debating the merits of repeating her request. Deciding against it, she finally turned to us.

One month — that's all we had to retrieve the amulet of immortality. Should we fail, she explained, the

Olympians would be at the mercy of Hades, and I would spend half of every year down in the underworld.

I glanced at the ornate calendar on the wall. It read October 16th. We had till November 16th--four weeks!

No pressure...not one bit.

Leo and Appolonia joined us midway through Athena's explanation of the route we needed to take.

"The amulet's location is known to only one being in the universe, and she currently resides in the Fields of Asphodel."

"Who's that?" I inquired.

"Medusa," Athena replied, her face tightening with worry.

"You mean the fields of punishment...figures Medusa calls that place home," Appolonia remarked.

"Fields of punishment? That doesn't sound too good." Leo shot a glance my way.

'It isn't. The fields of punishment," she continued, "was where the Olympians sent beings who created havoc on earth. Supposedly, you were tormented by that which you used to torture others."

'Tough place, " Leo interjected. "What I don't understand, though, is why Medusa is the only one who knows the amulet's location. Aren't you, Athena, like, the all-knowing Olympian? How come you don't know where it is?"

Athena raised her right eyebrow, a sign she wasn't pleased with Leo's challenge of her.

"It's not that simple, " she replied. "Medusa was the daughter of the Titans, Porcys and Ceto. She was the youngest and her father's favorite. Porcys knew the location of the amulet and told his daughter. Even the Olympians do not know its whereabouts."

A knock on the door interrupted Athena. Hermes walked in holding an oversized map. "Good...you're all here."

He spread it across the table. Greek words dotted the large manuscript.

"The map of Mephistopheles...nice work!" Athena remarked. "How did you get it?" she asked, stepping closer

Hermes smiled and said, "The Helmet of Invisibility comes in handy, even down in the realm of Hades."

"No way...invisibility—where can I get one of those," Leo asked eagerly.

"Leo, let's focus on the matter at hand, " Hermes replied.

We crowded around the ancient document, eager to get a glimpse. It looked like a prehistoric treasure map. I searched for Tartarus, hoping to know enough Greek to find it. My Greek was good enough to spot the word in the upper right hand corner:

Τάρταρος.

And then it disappeared.

"Whoa, what just happened?" I asked.

'The location of Tartarus constantly shifts, so as to elude any mortals from entering without having earned it," Hermes explained.

"Earned?" Appolonia said.

"Death, " Hermes continued," is a welcome end for some mortals.

"Tartarus is a place for the wicked," Trinity remarked. "It is no place for the living."

'That is correct," Hermes said. "But there are times in the year when we can try and predict its whereabouts."

"So where'd it go?" Leo asked.

"Wait for it…"

We focused our attention on the map before us, waiting for the location of Tartarus to reappear.

And then it did.

"Oh, no!" Athena exclaimed. I followed her eyes and spotted Tartarus right next to the land of the Amazons.

Chapter 8

The Land of the Amazons

O ur twin turbo jet sped us along at four hundred miles an hour. We were all buckled in tight. Trinity sat to my right. Leo and Appolonia were behind us. I was trying to get used to the fact that a computer was flying the plane. Then again, I was bringing a robot with me so why was it so strange that a machine was the pilot.

I glanced over my shoulder. Janus stood quietly in the back.

"Altitude, 20,000 feet and climbing. Please remain seated until we stabilize."

"Any idea when we arrive, Cassandra?" Trinity asked.

"*Estimated time of arrival is in three hours.*" Cassandra replied. "*Leo, please put your seatbelt on until I tell you otherwise.*"

"Hey...how did you know? You got video cameras in here?" Leo sat back down searching for whatever gave him away.

"*My sensors detected a slight shift in the air molecules around you,* "Cassandra explained. "*I concluded that you were about to stand up.*"

"Can't compete with that! " Leo exclaimed, clicking himself back into the seat.

It felt good to have Cassandra back with us. We hadn't seen her since we defeated Gideon Nefaris. She was like a mechanical older sister, one I liked being around.

Appolonia read from a book with creased leather binding. It was as big as her.

"You have to listen to this," she exclaimed, turning the page eagerly. *In Greek Mythology, the Amazons are a warrior tribe composed of fierce women, not unlike the Valkyries in Norse mythology.*

She looked up with a smile and said, "How cool is that!"

"I guess...if you like beefy women," Leo replied.

Appolonia frowned in a comical sort of way. "That's not the point silly. Don't you like strong women?"

Leo blushed slightly. "Uhm... of course I do."

"It's not what you think," Trinity replied. "Mythology aside, the Amazonians do not like trespassers—male or female. They will cut us down just as they would Samson and Leo, and they will block our passage into Tartarus with all the ferocity at their disposal"

"There is another option other than fighting," I interjected. "I remember reading a story involving Hercules. Cassandra, please search known weaknesses for the Amazonians."

"*Searching...According to the myth, Hercules was the only one who has ever been able to weaken the warrior females.*"

'That's right!" I remembered suddenly. "He stole Hippolyta's belt."

Trinity shot me an incredulous look. "You want to steal the belt off the Amazonian queen? You're joking right?"

"Cassandra, who wears the queen's belt now?" I asked, paying little attention to Trinity just then.

"Searching...Hippolyta's daughter, Penthesilia, now possesses the Belt. This signifies a change of leadership in the not to distant future.

"What' so special about this belt anyway" Leo chimed in.

"Hephaestus forged it out of pure adamantium, the strongest metal on earth," I explained. "It grants the wearer incredible strength. Without it, I think Penthesilia will be powerless."

"And without their queen," Appolonia exclaimed, "the warrior tribe will not put up a fight...it makes sense."

I glanced at Trinity. She was the one that needed to okay my plan if we were going to run with it. Without her, it couldn't work. The creases on her brow told me she was thinking seriously about our options.

"I think it can work," she finally said. "But how are you going to get it from her?"

"Touching down in Themiscyra in five minutes."

"I'll figure something out," I replied.

I knew we were headed into unknown territory, but given what we understood about the history of the Amazonians I had a hunch the solution to our problem would come from Hercules and his legend.

We landed in the midst of a canopied forest, in a clearing by a narrow stream that looked good enough to drink. The plane's doors slid open. We stepped out.

It was late morning as the equatorial sun blazed in the early October sky. An engine revved from within the tail end of the plane. Out came a mid-sized truck the color of dark green.

"Jump in!" called Cassandra from the truck's interior.

"Getting through those trees is gonna be challenging, Cassandra," Leo observed as he surveyed the dense landscape in front of us.

"I would not worry about that."

Two metal doors above each headlight slid open. Out emerged two whirring blades that looked like they could cut through brick, let alone bark

"Compliments of Hephaestus."

"Satisfied?" Appolonia asked Leo.

"Time will tell," Trinity remarked. "Keep a sharp eye out. It isn't the trees we have to worry about. "

We piled in. A moment later our computer navigated truck was cutting a path towards the Amazons, and towards what we hoped would be the entrance to Tartarus.

It wasn't long before my instincts started to go wild. It felt like my head was on fire. Something or someone was out there.

"Do you hear that?" Trinity exclaimed.

Suddenly, the sound of low murmuring rose up all around us.

"Cassandra, stop the car! " I demanded. We jumped out, and I scanned the immediate area again hoping to spot where the sounds were coming from. I couldn't see anything different.

A-MA-ZO-NIA! A-MA-ZO-NIA! A-MA-ZO-NIA

We huddled together against what was a rising chant emerging out of the dense fauna surrounding us.

And then, the jungle in front of us transformed. What seemed like trees at first glance were now six foot tall female warriors that could hold their own with the Incredible Hulk. Glistening in gold armor, there were at least fifty fierce female warriors suddenly standing in front of us.

A voice emerged from the very center of the throng. "NO MAN ENTERS THEMISCYRA AND LIVES TO TELL ABOUT IT!"

The soldiers parted, and up walked a woman a head taller than the rest. Flowing blond hair fell to her shoulders. She wore a golden helmet, the type used by ancient Greek warriors. In her left hand was a spear the length of a medium sized car. To her right was a younger version of herself wearing a belt that radiated light.

"WHO DARES ENTER THE LAND OF THE AMAZONS?" she exclaimed, stepping towards us ominously. In lockstep with their leader, the warriors behind her took a step forward.

It was obvious who stood before us: Hipployta, the queen of the Amazons.

Trinity shot me a glance as if to say--we were in for a fight so get ready.

But I had another idea in mind.

"My name is Samson Turner and these are my friends. We mean you no harm." I paused, trying to get a sense of Hippolyta's next move. She stood there, stone faced and ready to attack. "The Olympians have sent us on an important mission."

"We know of your quest, heir of Hercules!" She replied, taking one more step towards us. The warriors erupted, chanting louder and louder:

A-MA-ZO-NIA! A-MA-ZO-NIA! A-MA-ZO-NIA

And then I saw her—

Discord!

With a malicious smile across her face, she emerged out of the throng and stood to the left of Hippolyta, followed by an older woman that looked strangely familiar.

"Hera!" Trinity whispered loud enough for me to hear.

"SEIZE THEM!"

Chapter 9

A Thousand Female Warriors

L ike the ancient warrior Achilles, Leo gained invulnerability when I dipped him into the river Styx to save his life. So it was no surprise then that when fifty or so Amazonians attacked us, Leo instinctually became a human bowling ball and just rammed right through them.

"HELP WOULD BE APPRECIATED RIGHT ABOUT NOW!" He yelled as a particular giant of a female was about to throw him up in the air.

"I'M COMING!" It was Appolonia running towards him. Twisted strands of ebony colored hair flew towards the Amazon holding Leo. One of them wrapped around the warrior's ankle and with the strength of five men picked up the fierce female and chucked her to the side like she was made out of paper. Leo gained his bearings quickly and then joined Appolonia in stemming the onrushing tide of Amazonians.

I went straight for Discord, knowing that if I could keep her busy our chances of surviving would increase.

"AAARRGH!" She ran at me with sword in hand and venom on her face. I tried to sweep her legs from under her but somehow she anticipated me. With a swift kick to my head I was on the ground, and she was standing over me.

"Pathetic mortals--always aspiring to be like us," Discord hissed.

A second later, she brought her sword down upon my head.

"CLANG!" It bounced off my right hand, a benefit I received when I dipped Leo into the thick, black water of the river Styx. To Discord's surprise her sword had just struck something metallic.

I jumped up swiftly. "If you consider yourself one of the Olympians," I replied, "than I'll take being a mortal any day of the week." Keravnos materialized in my hand, and I lunged at my foe.

I brought Keravnos crashing down on her shield, knocking her off her feet. Swiftly I brought my sword to her throat. I had the upper hand now.

Trinity was holding her own with three hulking Amazonians. Behind her, Leo was attempting to free himself from the grasp of a female that stood two feet above him.

"ENOUGH!" A voice yelled.

It was Hera. She held Appolonia by her hair.

"YOUR VAIN ATTEMPTS TO BATTLE YOUR SUPERIORS IS FUTILE. DESIST NOW!" she commanded, her flowing white robes in contrast to her steely face.

There was nothing else to do. I knew from the history books that Hera had a reputation for cruelty. We could not risk Appolonia's life.

Trinity gave up the fight. I dropped Keravnos.

"For once a mortal does the wise thing," the queen of the Olympians sneered. "Take them!"

Not one Amazonian moved.

'My warriors respond to no one but me, Queen," declared Hipployta.

Appolonia giggled.

"SILENCE YOU IMPUDENT GIRL!" Hera's eyes flashed in anger.

She turned to face Hippolyta. "Order your troops to follow my command, or our working relationship will not be....shall we say... productive."

The queen of the Amazonians grimaced slightly. "As you wish," she replied, clapping her hands twice. Immediately, they grabbed us.

Twenty minutes later, we were marching in single file through the jungle. Cassandra was left behind.

We walked and walked, trudging through the loose soil of the jungle until, by degrees, I saw a pyramid like structure appear on the horizon. An opening in the dense thicket gave us a clearer view of what lay in store for us.

As far as the eye could see Amazonians in all shapes and sizes blanketed the expanse that opened up in front of us. There must have been a thousand wild-eyed women warriors practicing, in synchronized movements, the best way to tear apart a human being. Beyond them, a cloud covered mountain loomed large on the horizon.

"MOVE IT! demanded a husky voiced soldier behind me.

"Hold on...I'm moving as fast as I can," I replied.

"By the Gods, you will move faster mortal or I will have your head!" She shoved me, and I stumbled down to the floor on purpose, taking the opportunity to scope out the area for a way out.

As far as I could tell there was none. I glanced at Trinity. For some reason she was looking up at the sky.

Did she know something I didn't?

The sun hung heavy in the sky. It felt like a million degrees. They led us towards the opening to what could only be described as the home of the Amazons.

Standing fifty feet high with stairs on each corner of the structure, it looked like an ancient Inca pyramid. The entrance was flanked on both sides by rows of immovable soldiers.

Hippolyta raised her hand suddenly. She turned to face us. The sound of soldiers marching came to an abrupt stop.

"Welcome to Themyscira, home of the Amazons." she declared, facing us. "You are our prisoners."

"Get used to it!" Discord hissed in my ear.

The cavernous entrance swallowed us up as we resumed marching in what seemed to be a gradual descent down into the center of the structure. In the distance, I heard the faint sound of water flowing. Torches, jutting out from the rocky walls, caused misshapen shadows to dance ominously around us.

We turned a dark and dank corner and soon enough our new *home* materialized. It was a cell no greater than an average classroom with a couple of beds and a table in the middle.

"Where's the bathroom?" Appolonia cried out. "There is no way I'm staying in there without a bathroom!"

Chapter 10

Jailed

I t was impossible to know whether it was day or night. Judging by the smell we were somewhere deep underground. We must have been there for a week, alternately sleeping, eating and thinking about ways to escape. So far, we had come up with one sure way to annoy the heck out of them.

"I NEED TO GO AGAIN!" Applonia yelled out through the iron bars. A few seconds later, a muscle bound Amazon holding a spear the size of a medium sized car appeared in front of us.

"Again! Will this madness not end?"

I could see the veins pop up on her forehead.

"A girls gotta go when a girls gotta go," Applonia declared.

"You mortal females are so weak. No wonder the males dominate you." The Amazon pulled out a serrated key from inside her belt and stuck it into the cell door. Appolonia stepped out, her thick locks standing on end like some wild octopus ready to do battle.

"Listen, you lame excuse for a woman," she hissed. "Don't compare us. It's insulting."

"GRRRR." The hulking female guard looked angry enough to eat Appolonia.

"Come with me!" the guard barked as she turned towards the opposite direction. "Be right back," Appolonia said, winking mischievously.

"That girl is amazing," Leo remarked in admiration.

"She's definitely brave," I added.

"Appolonia irritating them is only going to get us so far," Trinity remarked. "We need to figure a way out."

"Right!" Leo added. He started to pace back and forth. "What if I, like, fake throw up so that the guards will rush in…then both of you can jump them."

"That's not going to work. Have you seen the size of those goons?" Trinity remarked.

"She's right," I added. "We can't do it using force. They'll overwhelm us."

Just then the sound of heavy footsteps caused us to cut short our conversation. Within a couple of seconds, Hippolyta , the queen of the Amazons stood before us."

"Hello. How may I be of service?" she said in a strange English accent.

Leo scratched his head quizzically. "Uhm... I don't know what you mean, your...uhm...highness?"

"Don't be so dense, Leo. It's Janus!" Trinity rushed towards the bars as the air around the figure of Hippolyta melted, and the shape of Janus, our robotic friend, materialized in front of us.

"You are such a sight for sore eyes," I declared excitedly. "How'd you find us?"

"Did you forget that I am attuned to your thoughts, Samson Turner?"

101

'That's right! Good old Hephaestus."

"I assume you would like to exit your unaccommodating accommodations?"

"Hurry…before the goon arrives," I yelled.

Janus's hand retracted backwards, and in its place appeared a contraption that looked a lot like a Swiss army knife. We heard the sound of a key turning, and then the door opened up.

"If you shove me one more time, I swear I'll…"

"Oh no! It's Appolonia …and the guard," Trinity whispered. "Quick, Janus, change back into Hippolyta."

"Puny mort—my queen!" The warrior female stood at attention. "No one notified me of your visit."

"I do not give notice to underlings. Stand aside!" Janus looked fierce as the Amazonian queen. Impressive! I thought.

We followed Janus up towards the entrance. Suddenly a voice inside my head interrupted my thoughts.

We need to get close enough to the real Hippolyta in order to obtain her belt, the source of her power.

Janus stared at me.

Follow my lead. When you have the chance grab the queen.

I nodded slightly. The light ahead indicated the exit. Get ready, I thought. This is going to happen fast.

The primal chants of the thick sea of warriors in front of us roused me into high alert. They were engaged in battle maneuvers, thrusting and parrying with ferocity. Their chant made my skin crawl.

Men want to dominate!
The Amazon will put to death!
Men want to dominate!
The Amazon will put to death!

I turned to Trinity and motioned towards my midsection. She seemed confused, but soon a look of recognition dawned upon her face. She gave me a slight nod.

Janus strode right through the Amazons who, thinking it was their queen, bent their heads in respect. I searched in vain for Hippolyta. Finally, I spied her standing by a poplar tree on top of a medium sized hill, her back to us. She was in heated conversation with a figure whose face was obscured.

Janus swiftly changed course and headed towards her. I knew we had only one chance at this.

I picked up the pace just enough so that we wouldn't raise suspicion. Janus, in sync with my every thought, did the same.

We had left the jail guard behind us now. Trinity stood to Janus's right. Appolonia and Leo were behind us. Her ebony colored locks stood on end in preparation for what was to come.

But the inevitable occurred. Soon enough we heard the ferocious shouts of soldiers. They had realized Janus was a fake!

"SAMSON, THEY'RE COMING!" Leo yelled. I broke into an all out run towards the Amazonian queen who, jarred by the shouts of her soldiers, turned to see what the disturbance was about. Keravnos materialized in my hand.

A figure emerged from the background, shoving Hippolyta aside, and let loose a fireball from her hands. "IT'S HERA! WATCH OUT!" Trinity yelled, pushing Janus and I out of the way. Without a moment to lose, I somersaulted in the air and landed in front of Hippolyta, holding Keravnos to her neck. "Call her off—NOW!"

"You are foolish, mortal, to come here in this way," hissed Hera, her hands crackling with white hot energy. "Just like your predecessor, the Hercules of legend, you will die a painful death...I will make sure of that."

"Yeah, yeah...sticks and stones may break my bones...," Appolonia chortled.

"You dare mock me! I will cut your heart out and feed it to the crows of Olympus!"

"The belt...now!" I demanded from Hippolyta.

"You cannot!" Hippolyta cried. "No man has ever taken the belt from the queen of the Amazons." The sound of soldiers marching grew until at least a hundred were standing behind us ready to spear us to death.

"One man has, "I said. 'Now hand it over...slowly."

"Of course," Hippolyta said, slowly stepping forward"...the heir of Hercules. I should have known better. Penthesilia, my daughter, come and witness the treachery of man."

The sea of soldiers parted and from within emerged a young woman no older than Trinity. She walked so softly it seemed as if she was gliding. Hair the color of a fierce sun with skin as white as chalk, she drew me into her emerald colored eyes.

"SAMSON!" yelled Trinity. "FOCUS!

"Huh..what!" I had been transfixed and almost let my guard down. Discord had stepped closer to me. Within a flash, Appolonia was there by my side, her wild locks waving around ominously. "Don't even think about it!" she threatened.

"I'll handle this!" Trinity declared walking towards the Amazon princess. "The belt, if you don't mind." A blank expression on her face, Penthesilia unclasped the golden girdle from the back and slowly gave it to Trinity.

"If this is going to work a man has to take possession," she explained, handing it over to me.

"What will you ask of us, heir of Hercules? We are at your command," Hippolyta stated with royal dignity. In one motion, the female warriors all around us bent down on one knee.

"We need access to Tartarus," I explained. "We know the entranceway is guarded by the Amazons.

"Children...entering the land of the dead on their own? Athena must be mad." Hera hissed.

"Take it easy, Queenie," replied Appolonia. "We know what we're doing."

"Be silent you foolish girl or I will turn you into a cockroach!"

"Good Queen Hera," Hippolyta pleaded. "The belt is no longer in our possession. I beg of you."

"Very well…come daughter, our time will come." A tiny, black dot materialized behind the queen of the Olympians. Within seconds it grew into the size of a circular door. Hera stepped in. Discord followed. And then they were gone.

"Enough of this! " Trinity interjected. "The location…now!

Dark clouds loomed large on the horizon. Dusk was approaching. Nighttime was going to make our mission that much more difficult. A week had already gone by and there was no more time to lose. We needed to speak to Medusa now.

"Ours is a sacred trust. We have never divulged the location of Tartarus," Hippolyta explained.

"The fate of the Olympians is at stake here, good queen," I offered, bringing Keravnos down slightly. "We do not seek the entrance for selfish reasons."

"Very well."

She pointed towards the horizon. "Over yonder at the foot of the mountain lies the portal you seek. But be on your guard, heir of Hercules, the way inside is filled with the madness of the dead."

"Thank you, good queen. Forgive us, but we will hold onto your belt until we reach the entrance of Tartarus. Once there, I will lay it down for you to retrieve."

Hippolyta nodded slowly.

"Let's go."

The belt in one hand and Keravnos in the other, I stepped away slowly as the Amazons parted to give us way.

Chapter 11

Tartarus

We walked for hours down into a dark and dank passageway lit by torches on either side. It seemed like time itself had stopped.

"I thought for sure the Amazons would chase us," Appolonia said.

"They wouldn't venture down into the realm of the dead," Trinity replied. "Their agreement with the Olympians ends at guarding the entranceway. That is all."

"What's the date, Janus?" I interjected.

October 23rd..

"We have twenty-five days left to gain the amulet."

Noted.

"We'll do it, Samson. Don't worry," Appolonia said from behind me.

"Thanks, Appolonia."

"I see something," Trinity suddenly whispered. There was some kind of opening up ahead, a faint light barely discernible. "I can't make it out so well...looks like trees," she continued, walking forward.

We stepped into a dark clearing. The air was thick with the smell of pine. From behind the trees a human form would emerge every so often only to walk towards another tree, and disappear behind it. We stood there in silence for some time, watching, trying to understand their movements. "The Fields of Asphodel," Trinity finally whispered.

"Who are these people?" murmured Appolonia.

"I 'm not sure," Trinity replied. "Wait a second--do you feel that all around us?"

The air seemed to be infused with moisture. It was as if we were suddenly walking through a wall of water.

Samson is correct, Janus suddenly observed. *The moisture level in the atmosphere is indeed quite high. It seems the hydrogen and oxygen molecules are quite close down here.*

"Will you get out of my thoughts, please," I demanded. "You're creeping me out."

Sorry. I thought since we're surrounded by dead people, it would be wise to sync with your thoughts.

"Yes...I mean...no...I mean, I'll tell you when it's okay."

Got it.

We walked ahead, into the field. The sky was grey and covered with angry clouds. A powerful gust of wind shoved us forward.

"Samson," Leo exclaimed, scanning the sky. "We're going to need somewhere to hide."

"I hear you," I replied, wiping beads of moisture from my forehead.

Then the skies opened up, and before we knew it we were standing in the middle of a massive rainstorm.

"WE'RE GETTING SOAKED!" I shouted. "LET'S FIND SOME SHELTER!"

"LOOK…UP AHEAD! IT'S A HOUSE…LOOKS LIKE A COTTAGE!" Leo yelled back.

Through the thick wall of rain, we saw a light coming out of a triangular shaped window.

"LET'S GO!" I called out through the downpour.

We darted towards the small house. Janus hovered beside us.

I banged on the door.

No answer.

I banged again, this time harder. We were drenched to the bone.

"IT'S GETTING WORSE OUT HERE!" Appolonia called out as she held onto Leo for support.

It was if the heavens opened up completely. Layers and layers of cascading sheets of water made me feel like we were in the middle of a violent waterfall.

"OWW!" Leo cried out. A cragged piece of ice hit him in the head. A second later, we were being pounded by hail stones the size of golf balls.

"THAT'S IT! WE HAVE TO GET IN THERE!"

I kicked open the door hoping that whomever lived inside would understand.

We barreled into the dimly lit house. I quickly shut the door behind us. A lone candle stood on a weathered wooden table in the center of the room, fighting the dark that seemed to want to swallow it up.

"We need a little more light here," Trinity said, holding her hands up in front of her. A second later a small ball of energy began to emerge until, by degrees, we had enough light to study our surroundings.

"Wow! How do you do that?" Appolonia exclaimed.

Trinity smiled. "I'll show you when we're not so…uhm…busy."

The room was practically empty save for the oak table, a single chair tucked neatly underneath, and a worn out shield with a faded crest of two interlocked swords lying beside it.

"Whoever lives here must be real lonely," Leo observed. Appolonia elbowed him. "Hey..."

"We're in the Fields of Asphodel, silly," she explained. "Everyone here is alone. That's the idea."

"What do you mean?" I asked.

"Well, I remember Plato somewhere explaining that the unfortunate souls who end up here haven't made any worthwhile human connections when they lived. That is their fate—wandering alone for eternity."

"That's so sad," Trinity whispered. The ball of light hovering between her hands flickered for a moment, and then started to diminish in strength.

"Something's not right," Trinity said focusing intently. "I'm having trouble sustaining the orb."

"Why? What do you feel?" I asked.

"I'm not sure...coldness...gloom." The light flickered once more, and then went out.

A click, and the room was illuminated by light coming from Janus's eyes.

"You could've done that sooner," Leo remarked.

Trinity had it covered.

It was then we heard a wail...and then steps outside the door. A voice suddenly boomed from the dark.

WHO IS IT THAT DISTURBS MY DAMNATION?

"WE ARE NOT HERE TO HURT YOU, "I called out. "WE COME SEEKING KNOWLEDGE."

HAHAHAHAHAHAHAHAHA! TO LEARN...FROM THE DEAD? HAHAHAHAHAHAHA!

And then it stopped, and the lone candlelight on the lone table began to glow brighter. Soon enough the shape of a man materialized at the foot of the door.

Chapter 12

Sisyphus Awakens

"I would offer you a seat," the man ghost said, hovering towards us, "but I never sit. Too much time on my hands."

"Who are you?" Trinity inquired, cautiously stepping towards the apparition.

"I was the first king of Ephyra, the most powerful kingdom in the known world...and the darling of the gods."

"This seems like a strange place for a favorite of the Olympians," Appolonia remarked, inching closer to Trinity.

"King of Ephyra...wait a minute—you're Sisyphus!" Leo exclaimed.

"Sisyphus...down here? That couldn't be." Trinity remarked.

I thought back to what Hermes taught us about the ancient kingdoms. Then it dawned on me. According to Greek mythology, Sisyphus was the king who was punished by the Immortals for loving cruelty, for killing and taking pleasure in it. The Olympians sentenced him to an eternity of unending labor. Every day he was to roll a boulder up a hill only to have it fall back as he reached the top.

Damnation, according to the Olympians, was an exercise in eternal futility.

It was Sisyphus who hovered in front of us now. The question was — what was he doing in The Fields of Asphodel?

"I made a deal with Zeus two thousand years ago to take care of the wanderers in these fields. It was the only way out of Tartarus. I could not--"

Suddenly he stopped abruptly. Slowly he floated to the ceiling, and then let out a deafening yell:

MHUAAAAAAAAAAAAAAAAAAAAAAAA!

MHUAAAAAAAAAAAAAAAAAAAAAAAAA!

I held my hands up to my ears to stop the piercing scream. The shrieking man-ghost brought us to our knees.

"JANUS – DO SOMETHING!" I yelled out. Before I even had a chance to finish my thought, Janus was charging Sisyphus, only to run right through his wraithlike form.

MHUAAAAAAAAAAAAAAAAAAAAAAAA!

MHUAAAAAAAAAAAAAAAAAAAAAAAAA!

I couldn't take it any longer! My ears were about to explode!

And then it stopped, as abruptly as it began.

"Holy Hermes!" Leo exclaimed, stumbling up from the floor. "I feel like someone just whacked me in the head."

"So sorry about that," Sisyphus casually explained as he sat on an imaginary seat in midair, crossing one leg over the other. "It's the only way I know how to maintain

119

order in the Fields of Asphodel. Wandering souls can get so belligerent."

"How bad can they be?" Leo observed, stepping towards the door.

"You'd be surprised. The souls that wander in the Fields are not harmless. They ramble aimlessly down here because their lives up on earth were devoid of purpose. They're just looking for an opportunity to focus that untapped energy."

Sisyphus started to hover upwards once more, laughing like an insane hyena.

HAHAHAHAHAHAHAHAHAHAHAHA

"Oh, no—not again! JANUS!"

Janus rushed forward and enveloped his arms around the ghost like frame of Sisyphus. He crackled with white energy until the mad ghost finally ended his wail.

"*HEY!*" Sisyphus yelled out in mid hover. "*WILL YOU TELL YOUR TIN CAN OF A BODYGUARD HERE TO STOP THAT? YOU KNOW I CAN'T FEEL ANYTHING. ALL IT DOES IS IRRITATE ME!*"

"Will you promise to control your wails long enough to discuss the whereabouts of Medusa?" I demanded.

If ghosts could panic, then Sisyphus did just that. He suddenly sped to the door and stuck his head right through, leaving his torso to offer us a comical sight.

A moment later he zipped towards me and said, "You mustn't say her name! If she hears it, she will come and then I will never hear the end of it: *Sisyphus, can't you do anything right? For Titans sake, Sisyphus, you only have one job here. Must I report you to Hades?* On and on it will go until I will lose whatever sanity I have left. Please for Zeus's sake, lower your voice."

Then sit...er, hover still, and tell us what we want to know!" I demanded.

"Fine!" The ghost floated back slowly, staring me down as if I had insulted him. He gazed at what must have been his fingernails for a second, and then said, "You must pass the Valley of Silence. Medusa sits by the willow tree. But beware. No man," he glanced at Trinity and

Appolonia, "or woman, has ever returned from the valley."

"Where do we begin?" Trinity asked.

Chapter 13

The Voice inside my Head

We left Sisyphus shortly after. He made us promise to put in a good word with Medusa if we saw her. And then he laughed uncontrollably again. We ran out for fear of busting our ear drums.

"Whew, I'm glad we're outta there!" Appolonia remarked as we stepped into the dark night.

I looked around. "I'm not sure it's going to get any better."

The wind howled in the night. Trees swayed under the power of the gale. I wondered if I had gotten us into a situation we couldn't handle. The Valley of Silence didn't sound like it was going to be much fun.

"*Samson,*" Janus said, "*The road we seek is a mile up, just over the hill.*" I squinted to get a better look but couldn't see anything, just darkness without end.

As if anticipating my reply, Janus remarked, "*Infrared vision helps. Not something mortals come equipped with, I imagine.*"

"Very funny, tin man, "Leo interjected. "Just lead the way."

"*Tin man…I will have you know, Leo, that I am constructed of pure adamantium. There is not one millimeter of tin in my frame.*"

"It's a figure of speech, Janus. Leo, didn't mean anything by it," I said.

"*I certainly can chill out as it is becoming increasingly frigid.*"

"Chill out means…never mind! Please, just lead the way."

Janus was right. The temperature had suddenly dropped. We needed to get going. Our robotic friend turned around and marched in the direction he had

124

marked out for us. We followed, cold and unsure of what lay ahead.

It was darker now. Light was diminishing at a rapid pace. I could barely see the outline of my hand. Trinity, Leo and Appolonia were nowhere to be seen, yet I knew they weren't far.

"LEO!"

"SAMSON, WHERE ARE YOU?"

"CLOSE BY!"

"WAIT THERE! I'LL WALK TOWARDS YOU!"

The last glimmer of light went out. I could see nothing. "CAN YOU STILL HEAR ME?" I called out into the blackness.

"SAMSON, YOU'RE FADING! I CAN'T HEAR YOU!

And then it was silent. I tried to call out once more, but no sound came out of my mouth.

And I tried again. Silence once more.

Fear crept up my spine. I was blind to everything around me, yet I *felt* something out there, something massive.

The air was thick and heavy. It was difficult to breath.

"Saaaaaaaaaaaaamson…"

It was a voice…inside my head…but it wasn't Janus.

"Saaaaaaaaaaaaamson…"

"Who are you?"

"Who am I? Hahahahahahahahaha! I am that which haunts you in the nighttime."

"Hades!"

"You dare come into my home on your puny quest!

"Get out of my head! Now!"

"Fool! Your fate was written long ago. The Olympians are finished. I will be supreme soon enough."

It was then I felt the air escape me. My breathing became difficult. I was struggling for breath. The last thing I remember before losing consciousness was a sharp tug pulling me forward.

When I came to I was lying among what seemed to be sunflowers — black, disk-shaped sunflowers. In the center, a red eye looked out. I glanced around. Some paces ahead, Janus was bent over Appolonia. To the right, Trinity and Leo groaned in semi consciousness.

The sky was grey. The temperature was warmer now. I rushed over to Leo and Trinity.

"Where are we?" Trinity groaned as I raised up her head.

"I'm not sure. Still in the Fields of Asphodel, I think. Leo, you alright?"

"I will be when I get the puke-like taste out of my mouth. Ugh! What is that?"

"Death…Hades to be exact."

I recounted what happened. They had all passed out as well. Lucky for us we had a robot bodyguard. Janus had flown us out to safety, wherever that was. It turns out infrared vision does come in handy.

"We need to get moving. It's not safe to stay here. Appolonia, you ok?" She stood up, rubbed her eyes and nodded.

I turned towards the thick mass of creepy sunflowers. "Can you travel?"

"Barely, but I'll manage," Trinity replied, staggering up on her feet.

We walked for what seemed like hours. I was starting to worry that we were lost.

"Are these flowers looking at us?" Appolonia inquired, as she poked one of them in the eye. In a flash, a vine struck out like a whip and grabbed her around the arm.

"HELP! HELP ME!" Appolonia's hair was locked in mortal combat with the weird looking sunflowers.

128

Leo ran over. "It won't budge! What should we do?" he called out. Another vine, tentacle-like, wrapped itself around Leo's waist.

Whatever this flower was, it sure was angry. I ran over to help but nothing worked. Soon enough, I was entangled as well. Trinity ran over. "Don't get any closer!" I yelled out.

The bloodshot eye in the center--if it was an eye at all—suddenly blinked.

And then it occurred to me.

"Aplogize."

"What?"

"You heard, Samson, Appolonia. You're the one that stuck your finger in its eye," Trinity interjected. "Apologize."

Appolonia crossed her arms in defiance. The sunflower tugged at her. "Fine, fine!" Appolonia peered into the red oval and said, "I'm sorry for poking you in the eye, uhm, red thingamajoo."

Suddenly, the vines retracted, freeing us.

The sky began to thunder. "Let's get out of here before it changes its mind," Trinity exclaimed.

"Good idea."

We ran and ran until it seemed we were out of harms way.

Lightning flashed across the sky. "Something up ahead seems different," I observed, walking towards a hunched form.

Chapter 14

We Meet Medusa

Trinity stopped abruptly.

The figure had long hair, thick like rope. The closer we got the more her ebony locks rustled.

"It's Medusa," she whispered, holding out her arms to block us from going further.

"You don't have to whisper, girlie," said a voice, low and angry. "I hear everything."

Medusa turned to face us, her hair rising on end for a moment only to fall back down in seeming fatigue. "I may be old but I'm not deaf."

'We're not here to hurt you," I offered.

"You couldn't even if you tried. Hehehehe…feisty youngins aren't you?" Like curious snakes, a couple of strands of hair stuck their heads up to assess the conversation.

"Uhm…maam? We need your help," I continued.

"What can be so important that you would risk your lives to come into the Fields of Asphodel?"

"We are looking for the Amulet of Immortality?" Trinity interjected. "We were told you knew its whereabouts."

Medusa paused for a moment. Then she turned back to the tree. "You are not the first to search for the amulet. Nor will you be the last. Be gone before I lose my temper."

Appolonia stepped forward. "Hey, wait a minute!"

"*HISSSSSSSSSSSSSSSSSSSSSSSSSSS!*" Medusa's snake hair stood threateningly on end. "*HISSSSSSSSSSSSSSSSSSSSSSSSSSS!*

Surprisingly, Appolonia's hair in turn, thrust forward in a flash, defending against any possible attack.

Medusa turned around to face her would be opponent. She stood. She stepped towards Appolonia, her menacing tresses advancing alongside their owner. Appolonia stood her ground.

As if a silent message was sent out, suddenly, the wandering souls began to walk towards us. I looked around and realized that a mass of dim human beings were set to converge on us any moment.

"Get ready," I said. Trinity and Leo nodded.

Medusa stepped closer to Appolonia, trying, it seemed, to get a closer look at her face.

What happened next surprised everyone. Medusa's snake like strands approached Appolonia's raven locks like long lost relatives. Cautious at first, the two heads of hair began to weave between one another in recognition.

'Who is your father?" Medusa demanded.

"Huh…what?"

"Be sharp now, girl! Who is your forebear?" She repeated in a heightened tone.

"I don't know—I'm an orphan!"

Like a doctor examining something closely, Medusa held up Applonia's chin. "Well…that makes sense."

She turned to face us. "In ten thousand years, no man has ever known the amulet's home."

The snake haired demigoddess shot a glance at Appolonia, and then said, "I will tell you the amulet's location, but you will never get out alive."

The half dead ghouls around us began to groan.

HAWGHHHHHHHHHHHHHHHH!

HAWGHHHHHHHHHHHHHHHHH!

By degrees they stepped towards us. "It has begun," Medusa whispered. She stepped close to us and said, "The amulet is in Egypt, in the pyramid of Khafre, down in the Pharaoh's tomb."

The ghouls moaning had turned into a rising shout.

"You must leave! QUICKLY!" Medusa cried out.

"SAMSON, WE HAVE TO GO…NOW!"

Chapter 15

Apollo Helps Us in a Jam

There was only one way out. And that was through the unending sea of ghosts that were about to swallow us up.

"FOLLOW ME!" I yelled, running headlong into the mass of lost souls. The temperature suddenly plummeted.

"IT'S FREEZING!" Appolonia called out from behind us.

"I FEEL IT TOO!" Leo called out.

Frost had begun to form on my arm. We had to do something fast!

"TRINITY CAN YOU HEAT US UP?" I cried out.

Without a second to waste, she thrust her hands in the air. A second later, an orb of light enveloped them. It grew bigger and bigger.

"It's warming up!—I can feel it!" Appolonia cried out. The ghouls around us, startled by the sudden heat, parted revealing a path formed in front of us.

"IT'S WORKING! LET'S GO!" I cried.

We ran on as fast we can. Trinity led the way. Behind us the mad ghosts gave chase, the cold biting at our backs.

"I CAN'T HOLD IT MUCH LONGER," Trinity yelled. She stumbled, and the lights went out. The ghouls thrust towards us sensing our weakened state.

Suddenly, I spotted something through the thick darkness.

"SOMETHING'S THERE—LOOK!" I called out. It was a hole, small at first but gradually widening.

It kept getting bigger, to rip the fabric of space itself, until it was big enough to fit even a person.

"APOLLO!"

The Olympian stepped out and lit up the place like a small star. The phantoms were scared. As if scorched by a raging fire, they retreated into the darkness.

"QUICKLY! THIS WILL NOT HOLD THEM FOR LONG," Apollo called out. "In here!"

I raised Trinity over my shoulder, and ran towards the light. We jumped into the portal. Appolonia, Leo and Janus followed.

I felt my head get sucked into a vacuum — and then I was on the other end.

Athena was waiting for us. She sat behind a large oak desk, her pet owl, Erasmus, perched on her shoulder.

"You have made it! Thank the Fates!" she exclaimed, rushing to greet us. "Apollo, you have done well."

"Thank you, sister," Apollo replied. "It was difficult to find them down in the Fields of Asphodel. I could not feel them. And then I remembered Janus. I honed in on his radio frequency."

"I did not know I emitted a radio frequency."

"Perhaps you should have a conversation with Hephaestus?" Apollo remarked.

"Never mind that now," Athena interjected. "We need to catch up. Please, come in and get comfortable. There is a delicious dinner prepared for you."

Suddenly, the door swung open, and there stood Esmeralda, our house mother from when we stayed with Polytitus. "Hello, my dears!"

Trinity ran to greet her, and Esmeralda enveloped her in her arms.

It was an hour or so later that we recounted our adventures. "My, my, you have been through quite an ordeal," Esmeralda observed. "Ghouls and Medusa…tsk, tsk, these Olympians will never get tired of their quests…but children…unconscionable!"

"You know we're not children, right Esmeralda?" I explained. "I'm practically fifteen."

"Hush now, Samson, and eat up. That goes for the rest of you, dearies. You make sure you eat up all those pancakes. I picked those blueberries fresh from my garden."

"You don't have to tell me twice, "Leo exclaimed. "I could eat ten of these." He stuffed a hulking piece dripping with maple syrup into his mouth."

'Thank you for breakfast, Esmeralda. I was starving," Appolonia explained.

'You're quite welcome. It's been too long. I'm glad to be back…and to meet you, my dear."

Appolonia smiled, revealing a mouth full of blueberries.

We sat in the middle of Epigosian's cafeteria, our conversation echoing slightly in the cavernous space. It was early morning, and school hadn't begun. Outside, the sun was barely visible above the horizon. Esmeralda walked back and forth from the kitchen, bringing Apricot Jelly Scones at one time, and heaps of strawberries another.

"Have you all had enough to eat?"

It was Athena. She had joined us without one of us really knowing she was there. We were too busy stuffing our face.

"Not yet," exclaimed Leo, forking another strawberry.

"Dude, you've had like twenty pancakes!" I observed.

'I know...it feels like I haven't eaten in days," he explained.

"Technically," Athena interjected. "You haven't eaten in fifteen days."

'Say that again!" Trinity put her fork down.

"You were in the Fields of Asphodel for fifteen days," Athena explained. "Today is Nov. 8th·

"How can that be?" Appolonia chimed in. "It didn't feel that long?"

"The Fields do not follow time the way we do on this plane of reality. The longer you're there, the more you feel time is limitless," Athena continued. "That is part of the punishment.

"Oh, no! That means we only have eight days left to retrieve the amulet!" I exclaimed.

"Yes, I was getting to that." Athena stood up. "Your quest grows precarious. Have you determined its location?"

"Egypt...the pyramid of Khafre," Trinity offered.

"Hmm...an interesting location. I wouldn't have thought it," she glanced at us and seemed to suddenly realize something. "Let us continue this conversation tomorrow. For now, you need some rest. Appolonia, you'll stay with Trinity for the time being. Janus, please visit Hephaestus. He has inquired about your wellbeing."

"Thank you, goddess. I will do that."

Chapter 16

Polytitus Visits at Home

"It's good to see you!" mom said, hugging me closely.

"You too mom." I hugged her back, glad to be home at long last.

We talked for a while in the kitchen. There was so much to tell her, but first I had to sleep. Fatigue was catching up with me.

"Should I wake you up for school?" she asked as I fell on my bed, clothes and all.

"Yeah…we still…have…."

Unable to finish my last sentence, I dozed off into a deep slumber.

The next thing I remember was Egypt, or in a place that looked like Egypt.

I stood in a vast dessert, a mile away from what looked like a pyramid. It was midday. High up in the Middle Eastern sky, the sun blared down at me. I looked around and saw a barren dessert wasteland.

Except for that pyramid.

I had to go and check it out. I just had to see what was in it.

And within a flash I stood at its steps. It was as if I had covered the distance with one giant step.

Suddenly, a stone door slid open. I stepped inside. Darkness enveloped me immediately, yet, somehow, I knew where I was going. The way was downhill, slanting right one time, and left another. I spotted a light flickering up ahead. Walking towards it, I began to hear voices.

"Hahahahahahahaha…finally it is mine!"

"Will you be quiet! You'll wake the Sphinx! Even *we* can not fight her off," the other voice demanded. It was a female, one who seemed strangely familiar.

"Wait a minute—there's someone here with us! I can feel him!"

I stepped back for fear of being recognized. There was nowhere to hide. A shiver ran up my spine.

I decided to run as fast as my legs would take me but the black void around me offered no possibilities for escape.

It was no use--they knew I was there!

"You have found your way into my psyche, Samson Turner!" the female voice hissed. "Very amusing, clever boy. We shall see who will laugh last. The heir of Hercules will soon find that it is dangerous to meddle in the minds of the Olympians."

A blinding flash, and my eyes opened up.

Knock, knock!

Mom's voice called out from the hallway. "Samson, it's time to wake up."

I was back in my room, cold sweat dripping down my forehead. That voice—where had I heard it before? Who was the man?

A nightmare…that's all it was.

Or was it?

I needed to get to Epigoisan and talk to Athena. I washed up quickly and headed downstairs.

Mom was in the kitchen. "Do you want some eggs?" she asked.

"That would be great. Thank you." I sat down and thought about the conversation mom and I were inevitably going to have.

"You were mumbling in your dreams last night?" she began. "You know Polytitus was here last week."

"He was—why?"

145

"I didn't expect you to be gone for so long. I was worried. You want to fill me in on where you've been for the last fifteen days?"

By the time I had finished telling her everything, I had eaten two plates of scrambled eggs and six slices of buttered toast. Mom was calm, asking me questions that probed further into the mystery of the amulet.

"The dream…whose mind were you in?" she asked, pouring herself another cup of coffee.

"I don't know. I've heard the voices before. I just don't know where. She said something about the minds of Olympians…called me the heir of Hercules."

"It could only be Hera," a deep voice behind me explained.

I turned to see a friend. "Polytitus!" I rushed over to greet my teacher. I wanted to jump and hug him, but his extended hand notified me he would do with a handshake.

"It is good to see you, Samson," Polytitus declared, his wide smile beaming from his stern face.

I shook his hand for what seemed an eternity. Suddenly, mom ushered him over to the table.

"How about some eggs, Polytitus?" she asked, already standing over him with a plate in hand.

"Thank you, Ms. Turner, but I've already eat— uhm,,,okay, if you insist."

I was so glad to see Polytitus. I knew he could help.

For you see, Polytitus was immortal, tasked by Zeus to protect the descendants sired by the union of the Olympians and mortals eons ago. To say he had a lot of experience was an understatement.

"Your mother tells me you've been through quite and ordeal?" he said. I shot my mother a look.

"I had to call him, Samson," she said in response to my silent questioning. "You screamed in your sleep last night. I was worried."

"It's okay, Mom...thank you." I turned to Polytitus. "Hera, huh. Why do you think?" I was relieved for the opportunity to talk about the strange beings I met the previous night.

"The queen of the Olympians has not been fond of those descendants of Zeus on the side of Alcmene," Polytitus explained. "As you are quite aware, that includes you."

"Yes…of course. The labors of Hercules…that was Hera's doing. But why would she join Hades. Doesn't she want to hold on to her immortality?"

"The only explanation I can presently offer is that she has made a pact with the king of the underworld to allow long life to a select number of Olympians, those I imagine who help Hades in his nefarious quest."

"Then it isn't just Hades and Hera we have to worry about?"

"I'm afraid not."

My mother poured me a glass of orange juice and said, "Drink that. It'll do you good." She turned to Polytitus. "What do we do next?"

"We have no time to lose," he explained. "Egypt is a land of ancient mysteries, and the amulet is but one. It will not be easy to find."

"But we know where it is," I interjected. "The pyramid of Khafre…the pharaoh's tomb."

"The tomb is just the beginning."

Chapter 17

Egypt Beckons

There was no time to waste. Whoever was involved somehow had found out the location of the amulet—that much Polytitus and I figured out. I ran upstairs to get a bag of clothes for the way. Whatever lay ahead of us in Egypt, I knew I needed a change of clothing.

"When will Trinity and the others get here?" I asked jumping down the staircase two at a time, a bag in tow. Polytitus waited by the door.

"It is just us this time, Samson...Athena's directive.'"

I glanced at him for a moment and said, "That's fine, but why? I would stand with Trinity against anyone, immortal or not."

"I know that," Polytitus replied, a half smile on his lips. "We can not take the chance. The journey is perilous enough for two."

"I understand." I struggled with a momentary thought. "For the record, I still think Trinity would be an asset."

"Duly noted."

The sound of running water came from the kitchen. "Give me some time to say goodbye to my mother."

"Of course."

I stepped into the kitchen. Mom was seated at the table looking at an old picture. I pulled up a chair beside her. "Who's that?" I asked.

She handed it to me. I saw a young couple in their mid-twenties holding a pudgy faced baby.

"That's us," my mother explained. "Your father and I a month after you were born."

I stared at the picture for some time. I had barely known my father, James Turner. He died protecting my mother and me from Gideon Nefaris.

My mother took my hand. "You know it would be perfectly fine with me if you told Polytitus that you can't go with him. I mean, we head somewhere else...away from all of this."

"Thanks mom." I squeezed her hand. "But I would never do that. I *could* never do that. I need to finish this." I stood up and gave her a big hug. "I'll be ok. Polytitus is with me."

"I know." She held me by my shoulders and said, "For some reason I don't wholly understand, I think that what you're doing can benefit many people."

"What do you mean?"

"This amulet you're after...hasn't it brought long life to the Olympians?

"Yes, it has."

"Well, what if you brought it back to be used by everyone, not just the Immortals?"

"You mean by human beings as well?"

Polytitus interjected suddenly by the door. "Samson, time is of the essence," He shot mom a strange glance.

"Please take care of yourself," she exclaimed and hugged me once more.

"I will."

Polytitus and I stepped out into the brisk December morning. Glancing back at mom, I thought about the question she asked — *What if you brought back the amulet so that it can benefit all people?*

It made sense: people would live longer, healthier lives. I flashed back to the way Trinity's broken leg was healed — immediate regeneration! The extracellular matrix embedded within the amulet would make pain and suffering a thing of the past. But what would the Olympians say? I searched Polytitus's face for some answer to my question.

"Our transportation has arrived," he remarked.

I decided I would give this more thought once the amulet was in our possession. We had nine days left to retrieve it.

At the curb stood a Hummer truck, the same one we used when battling Nefaris. The door opened and a familiar feminine voice greeted us.

"Welcome, Samson."

"It's good to see…er…hear you again, Cassandra."

"Set coordinates for Millers Field, thirty miles north of New York," Polytitus requested as the doors slammed shut.

"Scanning…estimated time of arrival is one hour."

"Millers Field? Isn't that an old airport?" I asked.

"Yes," Polytitus replied. The engine turned over.

"Are we taking a plane?" I continued, trying to get a sense of where we were headed. I was no longer the kid who would follow blindly. I needed to know the specifics of a quest.

"Yes. We are heading into the Middle East."
Polytitus said no more after that, and I decided not to push it. He must have his reasons, I thought. Cassandra sped away.

An hour later we pulled into a deserted field. In the center was an airstrip amidst vast swaths of wheat on either side.

'Where's the plane?" I asked, squinting under the noon day sun.

"It is already here," Polytitus replied.

Suddenly, I heard the sound of gears turning and metal scraping. I turned to see the Hummer transforming.

"Hephaestus has been working on a very interesting new idea," Polytitus explained. "He calls it, Multi-Metallics, metal structures that can change shapes according to need. He contends that it will revolutionize travel and conservation."

The Hummer had completely changed into a two-seat propeller plane. "I think he's onto something there," I quipped.

The door swung open. Polytitus stepped towards it. I hesitated. "I'm not sure about this. Egypt is a long way off, and that plane looks way too small."

"Rest assured, Samson Turner," Cassandra's voice called from within the cockpit. *"This Pilatus PX-6 is completely safe."*

"Besides," Polytitus interjected. "It's the fastest way into Egypt."

"What about teleportation? It worked before."

"Hera would know immediately. We can not take that chance." Polytitus flipped the switch to start the propellers. The engine roared to life as the blades gathered speed. I had no choice, I thought as I stepped into the plane. I had to follow him.

The door automatically closed behind us. Suddenly, the sky darkened. Thunder boomed across the heavens.

"You sure about this, Polytitus?

"Do not worry, Samson Turner," Polytitus remarked. "It is only Apollo creating a diversion for us."

Cassandra proceeded to roll down the field. She gained speed, and then, we were airborne.

The sky crackled with lightening. The wind howled. Egypt, the land of pharaohs and mummies, beckoned us towards her.

Chapter 18

Cassandra Steers a Storm

"*Estimated time of arrival is forty-five minutes,*" Cassandra informed us.

Rain slammed against our plane, jostling us back and forth in gut wrenching turbulence.

"Apollo has some sense of humor," I quipped, holding my stomach to quell the nausea I was starting to feel.

"It can't be helped," Polytitus replied. "It's the only way of entering Egypt undetected."

"How would Hades know?" I asked. "I mean, isn't he all the way in the depths of the earth?"

"Death and its servant look on all things, Samson Turner," Polytitus replied cryptically.

Suddenly, the sky flashed lightning, and thunder exploded in the air.

The plane lurched downward. I gripped the seat handles tightly. Polytitus clutched the steering wheel and pulled up.

Soon enough, the plane levelled off.

"Cassandra, what happened?"

"The right propeller is damaged!" I looked up— it was hanging by a thick rope like wire off the right side!

"Stabilize it--now!"

"Will do!"

The sound of gears turning filled the cockpit. I stared out my right side window—a massive glider had slid out.

"Cassandra, gliding in this weather is risky!" Polytitus exclaimed.

"It is our only option. The engines are both working. We have a 65% chance of success."

"Samson, brace yourself!"

Polytitus swung the wheel to the right, reeling down until, dimly, through what was now a gathering sand storm, Egypt's night lights became visible.

The plane shook until I thought the bolts were going to come off.

"Up ahead—look!" I cried out. It was a pyramid, barely discernable through the thick haze.

Outside, the sandstorm slammed against us. It sounded like millions of small rocks hitting us in every direction.

"Hang on!" Polytitus demanded. I braced myself for impact.

The next thing I remembered sand was spilling into the cockpit at a rapid pace. I looked around. Polytitus lay unconscious a foot away from me..

"Uuhhh…" My teacher's head shifted to one side. I unbuckled and forced my way through sandy grit that was threatening to drown us.

Quickly, I unsnapped his belt, pulled him off the seat and towards the door.

"CASSANDRA! CAN YOU HEAR ME?" A crackle and then the dashboard flickered on and off.

"CASSANDRA, IF YOU CAN HEAR ME—YOU MUST OPEN THE DOOR! I CAN'T GET TO IT!"

The dashboard flickered on and off once more. Sand was now at my neck—we were going to be buried alive within seconds if Cassandra didn't act!

The whirl of a gear, and then, suddenly, the door opened. We tumbled out and into the scorching Egyptian desert.

Sand assaulted us in every direction. As far as the eye could see, tiny specks of sand whirled around to form what looked like a massive desert typhoon. I needed to do something or we were going to be in some serious trouble. Cassandra was out of commission, and Polytitus was semi-conscious. I stood up and surveyed the position in which we found ourselves.

Suddenly, barely discernible through the sand storm, a vague structure materialized far in the distance.

"POLYTITUS, WAKE UP!" I yelled out. There was no time to waste. He groaned, and then, opened his eyes.

"Where are we?"

"THERE'S NO TIME NOW!" I called out. "CAN YOU STAND? WE HAVE TO GET OUT OF THIS SAND STORM." I lifted him on his feet and headed towards the structure that promised us refuge. It was our only option.

I placed Polytitus on my shoulder and headed to what I thought was our only hope.

Trudging through the sand, against the maddening storm, it seemed we were never going to reach safety. But then, it appeared—a massive structure standing fifty feet high with a lion's body and a woman's head.

It was a Sphinx! I rushed towards it in the hope of finding cover.

"Steps...head towards...the steps." Polytitus struggled to utter. I saw it—to the right of the belly lay a passageway.

A minute later we were in what looked like a tomb. I positioned Polytitus in a safe spot for now.

"You O.K.?"

"Yes. Thank you, Samson." Polytitus brushed the sand out of his hair. "Even an immortal has his limitations," he said. "Where are we?"

"Somewhere in Egypt...in a Sphinx," I replied. "...a massive stone one."

Polytitus looked around, reached out and ran his palm over the tan colored brick that was everywhere around us.

"Must be the Sphinx of Giza," he explained a moment later as he examined the dust between his fingers. "It will do…for now."

"What about the Pyramid of Khafre? That's where the amulet is."

Without saying a word, Polytitus pulled out a pocket sized piece of paper and then proceeded to unfold it.

"The map of Mephistopheles!" I exclaimed.

"Courtesy of Hermes," Polytitus explained, closely examining the caramel colored map. "Here…a passageway that runs from the Sphinx to the underground tomb within the Pyramid of Khafre. That is where we must go." He folded the map and placed it into his pocket. "This way," he said, and headed down the dimly lit corridor.

Chapter 19

The Sphinx

The pathway led us to what seemed to be an endless winding maze. We walked for hours unsure of out final destination.

At length, we came upon a clearance lit mysteriously by a lone torch. Suddenly, I spied odd shaped text on the wall. "Abu-Al-Haul...The Terrifying One," I said, reading from the time worn inscription on the limestone wall.

"What is that you're saying Samson?"

"The name of the Sphinx...in Hieroglyphics... it means the terrifying one."

"Interesting… I didn't know you read Hieroglyphics ," was all I heard Polytitus say as he continued his descent.

"Apollo's class…he often spoke about his travels in ancient Egypt…taught us the language to better understand the culture." I ran to catch up. The tunnel was narrower now, and heading ever downward.

I followed Polytitus for some time until, when it seemed there was no end, he paused suddenly, took out the Map of Mephistopheles and examined it closely. Turning to the wall and running his palm over it, he said, "It should be right here."

He pushed a section of wall directly in front of him. The sound of gears turning filled the narrow passageway, and then a door sized portion of the wall moved backwards, revealing steps that wound down into a cavern with no perceptible bottom.

Polytitus stepped down.

Hesitatingly, I followed.

The wall closed behind us. "It seems we are heading into the center of the earth," I quipped as we followed the winding way, step by step into the silent abyss.

"No, not the center...but close," Polytitus replied cryptically.

And then I heard what seemed almost impossible.

ROARRRRRR!

"Was that a lion?"

"So the legend is true," Polytitus remarked to no one in particular. "Hurry, we are very close now."

"Wait a minute—what was that?"

Polyitus turned to me and explained, "It is the Sphinx."

"You mean the actual half-lion-half human creature? That's real?"

"The Sphinx predates the Olympians. It is part of the history of this ancient land. We have no power over its primeval magic."

I searched my mind for what I knew about the sphinx. "Isn't there something about a riddle?" Hermes class on mythological creatures came to mind. I knew paying attention in it would come in handy one day.

"Yes, the creature is bound by the ancient ways to present us with a riddle."

"What will it ask us?"

"I do not know. The enigma of times past was about the changing nature of man," Polyitus explained. "Be ready for this. It must let us pass if we are to reach the Pyramid of Khafre." I nodded. He continued downward.

The end was in sight now. Light from a source I could not see nor imagine lit up the way ahead of us.

"What was it Hermes described? Yes, I remember now—what creature crawls on four feet in the morning, two at midday and three at twilight?" I recounted.

"Man—because he is a babe in the early days of life, stands on two feet in his manhood, and needs a cane as he ages."

"That is it," Polytitus replied, slowing his descent. "The ancients however tell of the shifting nature of this riddle. There is no reason to believe that she will ask us the same one. "

As we neared the bottom, there appeared on the floor bleached white objects, roughly shaped and strewn around in no apparent order. Polytitus saw them as well.

Bones.

And then it occurred to me—the sphinx would present a riddle to the traveler requesting passage. If the riddle was answered, the sphinx would give way, but if not, the traveler was dinner.

ROARRRRRR!

Had to think fast. We were steps away from meeting our inquisitor.

"Come into the light that I may gaze upon you," a woman's voice called out from the darkness. I glanced at Polytitus. He nodded. We turned into a courtyard of sorts, with statues of what must have been bygone pharaohs lining each corner. In the center, a creature, half woman, half lion sat staring at us.

The Sphinx!

Polytitus stepped forward. "We mean you no harm," he called out. "We search for the amulet of Immortality."

She had long lashes with eyes that glowed red. Her shoulder length mane was the color of deep night, and fell on a lion's torso covered by a rich brown fur.

"Many have searched for such an amulet," she replied. "None have succeeded. Come closer that I may see you better." Her voice took hold of me. I stepped towards the strange creature. Quickly, Polytitus grabbed me. "Be careful. She will transfix you if you are not vigilant."

Suddenly, she let out a deafening roar, her woman's head shaking like an angry lioness. "FOOL--THERE IS NO ESCAPE FROM ME! YOU HAVE ENTERED THE PLACE FROM WHENCE NO ONE RETURNS."

She stood up on all four legs, licked her lips, and stepped towards us, her head down as if preparing for battle.

"The ancients tell of a riddle that you must grant!" I blurted out.

She paused. Slowly she sat back down on her hindquarters.

"What do you know of the ancient ways, boy?"

"I know enough."

"Very well. If that is how you wish to die, so be it." She raised her head, and for a moment it seemed to me filled with a strange form of dignity. Her blood shot eyes went dark.

She began to speak.

"What is it that is beaten, becomes bent and broken, yet rises up and remains straight in its purpose?"

I glanced at Polytitus. His furrowed brow indicated he was thinking hard. I racked my mind for an answer.

It seemed like we stood there for hours, both of us straining, trying to find an answer to the riddle of the sphinx, yet not coming closer to solving the enigma.

"Truth," Polytitus finally said. "The answer to your riddle is truth. It is only truth that can be beaten, become bent and broken, and yet rise up and be straight in its purpose."

The Sphinx slowly stood up on all four legs. His eyes glowed red. "You are correct."

Suddenly, to my right the walls slid open. Out stepped Sphinxes identical to the one in front of us, four in total.

"You are correct," the first Sphinx said, approaching us. "But you will not leave here alive."

Chapter 20

The Amulet of Immortality

"Samson, Samson wake up!" a voice called out to me from what I thought was miles away. I opened my eyes. Polytitus was bending over me. "Finally! Thank the fates you are well!"

My head felt like it was hit by a hammer. I rubbed my eyes to get a better picture of where we were. Bricks upon bricks stacked thirty feet above me indicated we were at the bottom of an old well. "What happened?"

"They hit you from behind. … Infernal creatures… they attacked us all at once."

I grabbed hold of the wall to stabilize my footing and felt a thin layer of moisture covering the stone.

Polytitus pulled out the map of Mephistopheles from his jacket pocket. "According to this, we are under the Pyramid of Khafre."

"The Amulet--it's close by!" I said, feeling around for a clue. "I hear water."

"Yes," Polytitus replied, putting his ear to the wall. "A river, it seems." The roar of a lion stopped us in our tracks. "Quickly, we must free ourselves. We are in danger!"

Instinctually, I punched the wall—again and again and again. Polytitus joined me, and together we hammered away at the brick until at length a space opened up.

"IT'S WORKING!" I exclaimed.

"A FEW MORE SHOULD DO IT!" Polytitus shouted, slamming the bricks with a final blow.

Suddenly, bricks gave way to light. The sound of rushing waters greeted us on the other side.

"ARE YOU SURE ABOUT THIS?" I yelled out, staring down at a twenty-foot drop into a raging stream. "THIS WATER DOESN'T SEEM TOO FRIENDLY."

"POSITIVE!" Polytitus exclaimed, suddenly taking a step into the angry waters.

"GERONIMOOOOOOO!" I yelled as I took the plunge after Polytitus.

Instantly we were swept downwards into rapids that zigzagged left and right like a wild, wet roller coaster.

"HOLD ON!" Polytitus called out. "WE'RE HEADED FOR A DROP!"

I emerged from a pool of water that shimmered in golden undulations. Treading water, I tried to get a sense of where we had landed. A vast cave stretched around us for miles. In the distance, I spotted the feint outline of a massive structure arising from the water.

"SAMSON, OVER HERE!" It was Polytitus. I quickly swam over.

"You all right?" I asked.

"A little waterlogged, but, yes, fine. Do you see that?" He pointed towards the object in the distance.

Polyitus swam towards it. I followed, diving down into the cool, clear water.

Suddenly, I felt different—energized, like a thousand volts of electricity were running through my veins. Before I knew it, I was swimming through the water at breakneck speed, diving and jumping through the air like a super charged dolphin.

"WHOOOO!" The water was unlike anything I had ever experienced. Thicker, it felt like silk to the touch. "DO YOU FEEL THAT?" I called out to Polytitus who was staring at me with a bemused expression on his face.

"Yes…it tingles…a bit. The amulet must be close."

We swam further until, by degrees, the structure that loomed in the distance became visible.

"Tekhenu—yes, yes, this is it!" Polytitus exclaimed as he picked up his pace.

"Tek-who," I asked, unsure of where Polytitus was headed.

"The Greeks called them obelisks," Polytitus explained, "but it was the ancient Egyptians who first built them. These master builders called them Tekhenu."

Four sides that met at a point, the obelisk stood twenty feet high. Strange characters were etched deeply into the stone. A mysterious glow emanated from within.

Polytitus swam ahead and climbed onto the obelisk. I hung back, relishing the feel of the water on my skin.

"Samson, stop fooling around. We have work to do."

"Not yet—this is amazing!"

"It is the amulet…embedded within this ancient structure. It infuses the water." Polytitus submerged his head and drank deeply from the water. "By the fates—it is nectar in which we swim!"

The drink of the Olympians—I was swimming in the water responsible for their immortality! No wonder I felt supercharged.

I swam towards Polytitus and climbed up. We had found it. The amulet was within our grasp!

"How do we get it out?' I asked, searching the obelisk for some sort of lever that would allow us entry.

"I am not sure," Polytitus replied. "I did not expect it to be encased." He ran his fingers over the strange lettering. "Early hieroglyphics...3200 BC."

"What do they say?"

"Let me see...*ye who shall believe...beings from up high... his name*...by the fates, it is true then!"

"What? What's true?"

Polytitus didn't answer. He stepped closer to the obelisk, lifted up his hands and then called out, "OSIRIS!"

The stone structure grumbled and then slowly broke in two, revealing our prize. I reached over and grabbed the amulet. "Finally, we have it!" But there was no answer. Polytitus had disappeared.

Chapter 21

Olympus Goes Dark

It was dark and cold. A fog, thick and opaque, swirled slowly around us.

"Where are we?"

"Olympus...it seems," Polytitus whispered.

"You sure? I can't see a thing."

"I know the feeling. It is unmistakable."

The dense cloud surrounding us slowly lifted, revealing a number of the Olympians seated in their great stone seats. We had materialized in the center, next to the Eternal Fire that had now grown dim.

It was Hades who I first noticed, sitting to the extreme left of the Olympians. A look of pure hatred on his face, I could feel his eyes boring right through me.

I glanced at the amulet for the first time. An eye within a triangle glanced back at me. It glowed gold. I clutched it tightly.

In the center of the Olympians sat Zeus, scowling underneath his great, grey beard.

'WELCOME, SAMSON TURNER!" Zeus stood up, one hand holding his massive thunderbolt. "Truly you are the heir of Hercules to accomplish such a quest!"

Hades stood up. "You have done it!" he said, holding out his arm. "Bring it to me!"

Suddenly, I was paralyzed. Something—somehow, was dragging me towards the Olympian.

"NO!" Zeus shouted. "YOU SHALL NOT POSSESS THE AMULET!" he cried. In a flash, a bolt of pure energy flew at Hades.

The lord of the underworld staggered back, momentarily stunned. Suddenly, I regained control over my limbs once more.

"YOU SHALL NOT PRESIDE OVER US AS KING!" Zeus declared as he slowly stepped towards his brother, his thunderbolt at the ready should he need it again.

"FATHER—THE OATH!" Athena cried out.

"Do not worry yourself, daughter," Zeus replied. "What will come is in the hands of the fai—

AAAAAHHHH!"

It was Zeus who was now on the floor, suddenly writhing in agony.

"Husband dear…" Hera, now standing over Zeus, looked down at him with a smug expression on her face. "You know the Oath of Tartarus is nothing to trifle with." She stepped over the Olympian king and walked towards his brother.

"TRAITOR!" Athena cried out. Hermes flew to her side. Apollo's hands erupted in flames.

"Now wait a minute," Ares called out, holding his hands out as if to negotiate a truce. "Let's not do anything stupid."

"It seems the time for decisions has passed," Hermes said, hovering two feet above the ground. "Hera has made hers."

"Childish fool! Who are you to judge me?" Hera declared. "Zeus is no friend to woman! Years of neglect I endured, of looking the other way when he was nowhere to be found only to have his misbegotten children sitting next me…" she sneered at Hermes. "NO, WHELP! YOU WILL NOT JUDGE ME!"

She extended her arm towards him. An ebony colored wraith, ghoulish to behold, suddenly materialized in front. And then another appeared; and then a third.

"BEWARE!" Athena cried out. "HERA HAS BARGAINED WITH DEATH ITSELF!"

The ghouls surrounded us, spreading out until, by degrees, we found ourselves in the center of an ever encroaching mob of phantoms.

"STAND BACK!" Apollo cried. He erupted in a human torch like blaze.

"POLYTITUS, WHAT ARE WE UP AGAINST HERE?" I called out.

"DEATH ITSELF IS CONTROLLING THE QUEEN OF OLYMPUS! IT SEES AN OPPORTUNITY TO GAIN!"

Keravnos materialized in my hand. Whatever Death had in store for us, I was not going down easily.

Apollo lit up like the sun itself, growing in strength and energy. Still Death's dark demons surrounded us, pushing us ever closer to the crowded center.

"MORE—WE NEED MORE BROTHER!" Athena cried out to Apollo.

"WHAT ABOUT ALL OF YOU?—YOU WILL BE INCINERATED?"

"QUICKLY," Hermes shouted. "UNDER HERE!" A force field formed around him. We jumped into it. "LET IT RIP, APOLLO!"

A small star had now turned into an all out nuclear reaction. I could barely see Apollo through the blinding light.

But it worked. The fiendish ghouls could not stand up against the sun gods power. Soon enough they retreated into whatever shadows they could find.

It was eerily quiet as we stood there facing our killers. Hera stood with Hades. Ares silently sidled up to his mother. Athena, Hermes and Apollo stood against them on my right.

"That amulet will be mine!" Hades hissed. A jagged black portal suddenly opened behind him. "You swore an oath, Zeus! Remember that!"

The lord of the underworld stepped into the portal, Hera and Ares followed.

And then they were gone.

"AAAAAAAHHH!"

"Father!" Athena ran over to Zeus. His face was contorted in anguish. "We must do something! He is dying!"

"What can we do? — the Oath of Tartarus is unbreakable!" Appolo said.

"AAAACK!" A shade of blue fell over the face of Zeus. Before our very eyes, it spread to his chest and then his legs. He was suffocating and there was nothing we could do about it.

"Samson, the amulet! Quickly!" I handed it to Polytitus. He knelt, swiftly placing it around the Olympians neck.

The eye in the center of the amulet turned white, radiating outward into a sphere that encompassed Zeus's whole being.

A ball of pure light had swallowed up the Olympian. I shaded my eyes from the glare. The amulet glowed like a small supernova.

"What do we do now?" I asked.

"We wait," Polytitus replied. "The amulet is of an ancient time. No one knows its workings."

"Death's door is not easily avoided," Hermes added. "…even for an Olympian."

Athena crumpled into her throne, waiting for the verdict of the amulet. Hermes and Apollo followed suit. I sat cross legged on the floor. Polytitus stood watch.

It lasted for what seemed like hours, radiating white hot energy around the body of the king of the Olympians. Was it curing him? Transforming him?

And then it stopped.

Chapter 22

The Olympians at War

"Ugghhh…" Zeus shuffled slightly.

"He is awake! Quickly!" Athena cried out. We ran over to her father. What we saw knocked me for a loop.

"That can't be Zeus," I said.

He was no longer the grey haired one I remembered. Brown, curly locks gave him the impression of being a hundred years younger

"It's him," Athena declared. "It's definitely him."

"Uhhhnnnn… where am I?"

"You are in Olympus, father," Hermes replied.

"What happened?"

"The Oath of Tartarus…there was no escaping it," Athena explained.

"The Oath of Tartarus…by the faiths! How then am I still here?"

"The amulet of immortality upon your neck broke the hold."

He took hold of the amulet, stood up slowly, and gazed at his surroundings as if it was the first time he had seen Olympus. Athena took his hand and led him to his throne.

"You are quite changed father," she explained, seating him gently on the place he had taken for generations.

Zeus felt his face. "Yes, it seems the lines of experience are no longer etched into my appearance." He clasped the amulet once more. "We have it—finally, the means to defeat death itself. Think of it daughter, we will never fear extinction again."

"Wait a minute!" I interjected. Zeus turned his fearsome gaze upon me, his face more fearsome than I remembered. "I'm glad it has helped you but we are the ones who retrieved it. It belongs to us—me and Polytitus."

"Samson!"

"No, Polytitus! I refuse to be the plaything of the Olympians any further. We didn't risk our lives just so the amulet of immortality can be used for selfish reasons."

"Samson, that is enough!"

Zeus held his hand up. "Let the heir of Hercules speak. Samson Turner, we will hear you."

"Whatever or whomever created that amulet meant it for everyone, not just for the Olympians."

Athena stood up. "What are you saying, Samson?"

"I am saying that mortals should benefit from its power to heal. Think of the good it will do."

"That is impossible," Apollo declared. "Our immortality is what separates us from the humans."

"Why should there be a separation?"

"Samson Turner, you bring up a contentious subject, "Athena said. " Sharing our gifts with the mortals has never been done." She approached her father. "Father, can we meditate upon this?" Zeus nodded slowly.

She turned to me and said, "But first, there is the question of making your soul whole once more." Athena removed the amulet from Zeus and walked toward us. She placed the amulet of immortality in the palm of my hand and said, "When you slumber tonight, wear this around your neck and you will be healed."

"But—"

It was all I could manage to say before Polytitus took hold of my shoulder.

"It is time to go, Samson Turner."

*   *   *

The sunlight streamed through my bedroom window, warming my face in the morning hours. I had slept soundly for the first time in as far back as I can remember. I clutched the amulet. Hades had disappeared from my dreams.

Voices filled the kitchen. I rubbed the fatigue out of my eyes. So much had happened, I thought. I threw on some clothes, ran into the bathroom to wash up and headed downstairs to see what all the commotion was about.

Trinity, Leo, Polytitus and mom sat around the table. "Samson, you're back!" Trinity rushed over and gave me a big hug.

"Good to see you, buddy," Leo said as he enveloped both of us in his arms.

"It's good to see you guys as well," I replied wrapping my arms around them.

Mom gave me a peck on the cheek. "How about breakfast? I just made a batch of chocolate chip pancakes."

"I'd love some!" Leo remarked, spearing the last remaining piece of pancake on his plate.

"Isn't seven pieces enough, Leo?" Trinity chimed in.

"Sure you can have some more," mom replied, rubbing Leo's hair good naturedly.

"I better get mine before Leo gobbles everything up," I replied, taking a seat alongside Polytitus.

"How do you feel?" he asked.

"Better...no nightmares, thanks to this." I clasped the amulet.

"So glad to hear it. It is an object of great power."

"Must it go back?" Trinity pleaded. "Even if we had it for just a little while we can help so many people."

I glanced at her. "Polytitus mentioned your request to the Olympians," she answered in reply to my silent inquiry. "I think it's a great idea. Why should they be the only ones who enjoy perpetual health?"

"Zeus has made it clear that now is not the time." Polytitus explained. "Olympus is in turmoil and a battle awaits us all."

"A battle…with whom?" I asked.

"Hades, Hera and their minions are gathering. Death has claimed their allegiance."

"What does it mean for us down here?" I asked.

"Olympus is fractured. There is no telling what will befall the earth?" Polytitus replied.

Silence fell upon the table. The thought of the Olympians—ancient, superhuman beings—at war with one another did not bode well for mankind.

"Well, "Leo chimed in. "I guess I will have those extra pancakes. You never know when my next meal will be."

We all chuckled, breaking the tension that had fallen upon us. I looked around the table and felt strangely at ease. Trinity's bright smile warmed my heart, while Leo's hijinks could always make me smile. Mom plated me a couple of pancakes. "Thank you," I replied, truly grateful for her care. Polytitus looked thoughtful, lines of concern deeply etched into his brow.

We had a long road ahead of us but, looking around the table that day, somehow, I felt better.

"Ms. Turner, I can't stop eating these pancakes," Leo said, spearing yet one more piece. We all erupted in laughter.

*** END ***

www.ingramcontent.com/pod-product-compliance
Lightning Source LLC
Chambersburg PA
CBHW071908220626
47052CB00002B/268